"You're Quite an Actress, Jordan."

His voice was deceptively soft, his breath warm and gently caressing against her cold cheek. His eyes hardened and he laughed mirthlessly. "God, what a fool I was."

Before she could react, he nailed her to the stone wall with the pressure of his body. Jordan responded with a sensual adjustment, and desire curled through her as he parted her cape, his hands squeezing her waist, his lips pressing hot kisses into her shoulder.

In a voice as hard and cold as steel he said, "You see, Jordan. The only thing that separates you from the others is the price you demand."

ERIN ST. CLAIRE

has worked part-time in commercial television, at one time hosting her own daily show. Well known for her fluid sensuous style of writing, Ms. St. Claire has written five novels within eighteen months after her first serious attempt at writing fiction. She is married to a former show host and has two children.

Dear Reader:

SILHOUETTE DESIRE is an exciting new line of contemporary romances from Silhouette Books. During the past year, many Silhouette readers have written in telling us what other types of stories they'd like to read from Silhouette, and we've kept these comments and suggestions in mind in developing SILHOUETTE DESIRE.

DESIREs feature all of the elements you like to see in a romance, plus a more sensual, provocative story. So if you want to experience all the excitement, passion and joy of falling in love, then SILHOUETTE DESIRE is for you.

I hope you enjoy this book and all the wonderful stories to come from SILHOUETTE DESIRE. I'd appreciate any thoughts you'd like to share with us on new SILHOUETTE DESIRE, and I invite you to write to us at the address below:

Karen Solem
Editor-in-Chief
Silhouette Books
P.O. Box 769
New York, N.Y. 10019

ERIN
ST. CLAIRE
Not Even
For Love

Silhouette Desire
Published by Silhouette Books New York
America's Publisher of Contemporary Romance

SILHOUETTE BOOKS, a Simon & Schuster Division of
GULF & WESTERN CORPORATION
1230 Avenue of the Americas, New York, N.Y. 10020

ISBN: 0-671-44515-4

First Silhouette Books printing July, 1982

10 9 8 7 6 5 4 3 2 1

America's Publisher of Contemporary Romance

Printed in the U.S.A.

Not Even
For Love

1

~~**eoooooooooo**~~

The man finished the champagne in the fragile crystal stem and set it on the silver tray deftly held aloft by a passing servant. The tuxedoed waiter paused momentarily for the man to avail himself of another glass of the bubbly wine, then disappeared into the chattering crowd.

Reeves Grant sipped at his fresh glass of champagne, wondering why he had even taken it. He didn't want it. Everything had suddenly gone sour. Even the world's most expensive vintage left a brassy taste in his mouth. Derisive green eyes swept across the august assembly of celebrities and VIPs, surveying it with tolerant boredom.

An aging but still beautiful French film star was strategically draped on the arm of her new husband, an oil tycoon from Tulsa, Oklahoma. West Germany's gold-medal-winning Olympic downhill racer was earnestly hustling a sulky, sensuous princess from a Mediterranean country, but she studiously ignored him. A New York designer and his "companion and protégé," both dressed in flaming pink tuxedoes, were entertaining a group of avid listeners with a malicious tale about a former cover girl model who had gained forty pounds and had come to them for a figure-camouflaging wardrobe.

All in all, the crowd were rich, famous, or important. Or a combination of all three. Or merely outrageously notorious for one reason or another.

Greeting them all with dignified graciousness was the host of the lavish reception. Tall, strong, and lithe of figure, he looked to be exactly what he was, a Swiss industrialist of incalculable wealth. His blond, blue-eyed good looks secured his position on the list of the world's "beautiful people."

Disobedient green eyes refused a cerebral command and unerringly moved to the woman standing beside the millionaire. She was dressed in a stunning white gown. *White,* for God's sake! he thought snidely.

Twenty-four hours hadn't dimmed Reeves Grant's memory of how beautiful she was. The one-shoulder Dior sheath was worthy competition for any other gown there. The opal and diamond necklace around her slender throat was as exquisite as any of the jewelry that bedecked the other women in the room, and its simplicity was almost virtuous by comparison.

Her hair came close to being styled too casually for the formal occasion. It wasn't loose and flowing as Reeves had last seen it. Instead it was swept up into a knot at the top of her head. But the secreted pins seemed to have a tenuous hold on those dark, thick, glossy strands, a few of which had already escaped their confines. With the least amount of encouragement—say, a man's caressing fingers—the whole mass would probably come tumbling down around his lucky hand.

Dammit! What in the hell is the matter with you? he demanded of himself. He had been suckered, but good. Yet, like some masochistic fool, he couldn't keep his eyes away from her. The question kept repeating itself in his brain: What had she been doing in that bookshop last night? Or better still, what was she doing *here*? Among all this? These people? With that man? The tiny modest apartment over the bookshop and this palacial reception room with its frescoed and gilded ceiling, its marble floors, its glittering chandeliers, had nothing to do one with the other. She didn't belong here. She belonged in that infinitesimal kitchen with its cheery percolator and the smell of fresh coffee. He could still see her curled up in the corner of that short sofa, one of the comfortable pillows hugged to her breasts . . . Damn!

Leaving the dregs of champagne, he set the glass on a small table. His Nikon camera hung around his neck by its thin leather cord, and he adjusted it now. He was so accustomed to the camera being like an extension of himself that it didn't seem incongruous with his evening clothes. The crowd, well used to being photographed, seemed not to notice the camera either as Reeves threaded his way through them, his eyes intent on the cameo profile of the woman as she shook hands with a Belgian diplomat. The man at her side had just introduced him to her.

She leaned over the man several inches shorter than herself and spoke courteously to him, though her words eluded Reeves as he brought the camera up to his expert eye. He adjusted the ring around the lens until the delicate features of her face sprang into focus.

She was accepting the diplomat's officious kiss on the back of her hand when the photographer snapped the shutter. The automatic flashing device on his camera startled her, and she turned her head in the direction from which it had come. Quickly, he rolled the focus ring again as her face now filled his lens. Her smile was tentative, shy, and self-conscious as he pressed the shutter release.

This time the flash hit her full in the eyes and she was momentarily blinded. A dark forest of lashes blinked over gray eyes several times before she could clearly see. The photographer slowly lowered the camera away from his eyes, green eyes that impaled her with a ferocious, accusatory glower.

Her gracious smile froze for an instant before it totally collapsed. The eyes widened perceptibly. The mysterious rings around the irises grew darker. A darting pink tongue flicked over lips suddenly gone dry. Then the lips formed a small, round, surprised O.

Reeves had seen that same expression of wonder and caution just last night. It had been raining. The thunder had echoed through the narrow alleys and bounced off the stone walls of the ancient buildings of Lucerne, Switzerland. Rain had pelted his bare head.

But suddenly the storm had ceased to matter. When

he saw her face through the glass door of the bookshop his other senses had rested while his vision reigned supreme, devouring her image.

"Oh!" Jordan Hadlock had exclaimed. In startled reaction, she crushed the heavy book to her chest as another clap of thunder shook the windows of the storefront. Then she realized that the rattling glass wasn't the result of the thunder alone. Someone was pounding on the panes of the door.

Perched as she was on the ladder leaning against the book racks, she could see the front door of the shop without obstruction. But when she had closed the bookstore for the night several hours ago, she had pulled down the opaque window shade. Whoever was now braving the thunderstorm and knocking peremptorily on the door was identifiable only by a silhouette outlined by flashing lightning.

The shadow's size and form deemed it male. He was pressing his cupped hands against the glass, trying to peer around the edge of the shade. Jordan heard him mutter an obscenity that had no right to ever be spoken aloud, no matter how softly, and then the pounding started again, more emphatically this time.

Slowly, her heart thudding almost as solidly as the fist on the glass pane, Jordan descended the ladder and edged around the bins of books and newspapers until she stood a few feet from the door.

A lightning flash revealed the large masculine shape standing with feet planted slightly apart, hands on hips. Her visitor was growing more impatient with each passing second. Tottering on the brink of indecision, she weighed her options. It would be dangerous to open her door this late at night to a man obviously already angry. Still, were he bent on some crime he would hardly have announced his presence so forcefully. Maybe he needed help. A medical emergency? He certainly seemed distressed.

Without waiting to talk herself out of it, she went to the door and pulled back the shade far enough for her to see out. The light from inside the bookshop fell on a broad chest with a cotton shirt now rain-plastered to it. The shirt was unbuttoned at the throat and her curious eyes traveled up the strong cords of his throat to his face.

Her eyes widened in feminine interest. While the chiseled features were set in a grim, perturbed expression, the face wasn't menacing. She was slowly taking in the firm chin, the long, slender nose, and the green eyes when a scowling eyebrow lifted over one of them in a silent query. It said: Well, are you going to stand there gawking at me, or are you going to open this door?

Yes, she was going to open it.

She dropped the shade, slid back the bolt, turned the brass knob, and drew open the door. Two bags, which had escaped her attention before, were tossed through the opening, barely missing her feet. She scrambled aside as her bare feet were splattered with cold raindrops when the bags thumped to the floor. One was brown leather, the other navy canvas.

The man barged into the room seconds after his luggage, turned, and slammed the door shut behind him. He spun around, ready with a scathing remark on her hesitation at opening the door, but the words died on his lips as he looked down at Jordan.

For long moments the two stared at each other, expressionless, without speaking, their only movement that of their eyes as each surveyed the face of the other.

A few, very few, seconds ticked by before their breathing became audible. His was light and rapid because of his recent exertion; hers matched it for reasons as yet undefined. The only other sound in the room was that of the drops of rain that dripped off Reeves and fell onto the tile floor.

Jordan tore her eyes away first and directed them to the floor, where a puddle was forming around the man's booted feet.

"Do you have a towel?" he asked without notice.

"What?" she croaked, unaccountably disconcerted and disoriented.

"Do you have a towel?" he repeated.

"Oh . . . oh, yes. I'll be . . . Just a moment . . ."

She fairly flew across the room, switched on the light in the stairwell, and scrambled up the stairs as if the devil were after her. She grabbed a towel off the nearest bar in the bathroom, realized it was the one she had used after her shower, tossed it onto the floor, muttering self-deprecations about her own stupidity, and reached into the linen closet for a clean towel. As a precaution, she picked up two.

As she plunged down the stairs, she caught herself up, consciously took three deep breaths, and then descended at a more careful, reasonable pace. What was wrong with her?

He was standing exactly as he had been, though his eyes were busy scanning the shelves near him. He tilted his head to read a book title, and Jordan noticed the rainwater running in silver rivulets down his neck into the collar of his shirt.

"I brought two. You look as if you may need them," she said, extending him one of the towels.

13

"Thanks," he said succinctly before he buried his face in the absorbent terry cloth. He held his head still for several seconds before he raked the towel over his dark unruly hair and then around his neck, whisking quickly past the deep triangle where his shirt was open. The thick hair on his chest was curled damply. Jordan quickly averted her eyes.

He looked down at the ever-widening pool at his feet. "You're going to have a helluva mess on your floor. I'm sorry."

"That's all right. It will mop up. Who—"

"Hell, I'm sorry again. I'm Reeves Grant." He stuck out his hand and Jordan prevented herself just in time from jumping away from it. For some unknown reason, it seemed terribly risky to touch him, even in a friendly handshake. She didn't know what threat touching him posed; she only knew physical contact with him would be dangerous.

And it was. She had swallowed the unreasonable caution and taken his proffered hand. The moment his fingers squeezed around her, the muscles around her heart constricted similarly, and for an instant she didn't think she would be able to breathe again. However, to her vast relief, her involuntary brain impulses took over, and she sucked in enough breath to murmur, "Jordan Hadlock." Though he seemed reluctant to release it, she pulled her tingling hand out of his grasp.

"Thank you for letting me in," he said.

"What are you doing out on a night like this? Were you looking for me for some reason?"

He smiled ruefully. "No. I wish I could say it was that simple. I arrived this afternoon—dusk really. I've never been to Lucerne and wanted to scout around before I checked into a room. I dismissed the cab, walked along the lake shore for a while, had a bite to eat, and then started walking through the old town. The storm came up and I got hopelessly lost." He grinned at her winningly, boyishly, abashedly, and she laughed.

"Don't be so hard on yourself. It's easy to get lost if you don't know your way around the old town."

"Yes, but I'm a jaded traveler. I've been all over the world and am reputed to 'know my way around.' You won't let it get out that I blew my reputation tonight, will you?" he whispered conspiratorially.

"I promise," she echoed his hushed tones. Then she asked, "What do you do that takes you all over the world, Mr. Grant?"

"I'm a photojournalist. Free-lance mostly. Sometimes I team up with one of the news services if one of their own men is unavailable."

Her eyes opened wide in realization. "Reeves Grant. Are you 'R. Grant'?" He nodded. "I see your photographs often. I read a lot of magazines." She smiled as she indicated the shelves with a sweeping hand. "Your work must be fascinating," she said.

He shrugged modestly. "Well, it pays the rent. Or it would if I had an address. I live in hotels most of the time," he said. "Anyway, I can't tell you what a godsend your store was. I've been wandering around out there in this rain for half an hour and then I saw your lights on. I couldn't believe the sign on the door. An English newsstand! A beacon on a dark night, the lighthouse amidst the storm," he said dramatically, and Jordan laughed again.

"Well, hardly that impressive," she said, smiling. "But I'm glad I was handy."

"Do you have a telephone? And can you recommend a hotel before I completely ruin your floor?"

"Yes to both." Turning to the counter with the old-fashioned cash register on it, she pulled a telephone from beneath it along with a well-used brochure. "Which hotel do you prefer? Any along the shore of the lake are excellent, if your budget—"

"I'm on an expense account," he said, grinning. "You choose."

"All right." She placed the receiver to her ear and then groaned, "Oh, no!"

"What's the matter?"

"The telephone is dead. I'm sorry. Sometimes when we have a bad storm . . ." Her voice trailed off as she looked at him mournfully.

He only shrugged again. "Don't worry about it. I'll find a room if you can direct me out of here."

"But the rain," she protested. "Why don't you stay a while longer?" The words surprised her own ears and his brows quirked again in amusement. Covering her embarrassment, she hastened to add, "It may stop soon."

He looked out the window at the storm, which was still raging. If anything, the thunder and lightning seemed to be increasing in ferocity.

"I'm no martyr," he admitted. "I'll stay awhile. Am I keeping you from anything?"

"No—I was only shelving some books." She gestured toward the ladder.

"Then I insist on helping while I'm here."

"No, it can wait. I—"

"I owe it to you," he said. "That is, if you don't mind my wet clothes."

She did, but not in the way he suspected. The fine fabric of his blue shirt was still damp and clung to the ridges of muscle and bone on his torso. His jeans, tight to begin with, were molded in much the same way to narrow hips and long, lean thighs.

"No," she said shakily. "I'm not exactly dressed for company either." Suddenly, and for the first time, she was made aware of her appearance. After she had closed the shop, she had eaten a light dinner, showered, and donned her most comfortable pair of slacks and a ribbed knit cotton sweater. She had drawn her hair back in a haphazard ponytail and secured it with a tortoiseshell clasp. Her feet were bare. And she was wearing no bra—a fact made crucial by the green eyes that traveled down her trim body. As if being alerted of his scrutiny, Jordan felt her nipples begin to pout beneath the soft pink cotton and she whirled away in alarm, willing them to return to their relaxed state.

Why wasn't she wearing one of her functional skirts or business suits? Her homey clothes only made this bizarre situation seem more intimate than circumstances warranted.

But the intimacy was there with a reality that bordered on tangibility. Already she felt a shiver of anticipation each time she looked at Reeves Grant. Anticipation of what? The whole thing was becoming absurd, and she was sure the chaos existed only in her mind. *He* wasn't aware of it.

Indeed, when she looked back at him he was kneeling down with the damp towel, mopping up the puddle he had made. "Please don't bother with that," she said as she ascended the ladder with an armload of books.

"I think my clothes have dried somewhat, and if I get

this water up, I won't feel so guilty about invading your store. Do you live here?" he asked abruptly.

She was stunned for a moment and suddenly wary. Then she remembered getting the towels. And with her casual appearance, of course, he would deduce that she lived here.

"Yes," she answered. "Upstairs there is a small apartment. I've been here for three years."

"Three years?" He seemed shocked. "You're an American."

It wasn't a question, but she replied as if it had been. "Yes. I'm from the Midwest. Three years ago I found myself at loose ends and went to London. Business associates of my father helped me get this job. There is a chain of these English newsstands throughout Europe, usually in smaller towns where American and British newspapers are harder to find. We, of course, cater mostly to English-speaking tourists."

"What happened three years ago to make you feel at loose ends?" It was as though he had heard nothing else, but had homed in on the one point in her narrative that she wished he had overlooked. She was tempted to tell him that it was none of his business and dismiss the subject immediately.

However, looking down at him from her place on the ladder, she saw the green eyes staring up at her, demanding the truth. One strong hand, with fingers sensitive enough to handle the delicate intricacies of his cameras, was resting next to her bare foot on the rung of the ladder.

She pulled her eyes away from his as she mumbled, "My husband died." Her shaking hands busied themselves with the books she was lining up along the top shelf. It was taking much more time than should be necessary to get them just right.

"What are you putting up there?" he asked, breaking a silence that was stretching dangerously long.

"Philosophy and religion," she said. "The current bestsellers go on the bottom shelves. The spicier the book, the lower the shelf." She looked down at him and smiled impishly.

He laughed. "Good merchandising," he said. "Here. This is all." He handed up the last of the books and she leaned down to take them.

At that moment another crack of lightning struck close to the small shop and after a sizzling explosion at each fixture, the lights went out.

"Jordan!" She had momentarily lost her balance, but his hands came up around her waist to steady her on the ladder. "Are you okay?" he asked in the sudden darkness.

"Yes," she answered breathlessly. His hands were warm through the thin cotton of her sweater. Cautiously, her feet found the now invisible rungs and she eased her way down until she had gained the floor. "I'm afraid your first impressions of Lucerne will be bad ones," she said tremulously. His hands were still firm around her waist.

"I'd say my first impressions have been delightful." His voice was vibrant and its intensity startled her. His hands moved up almost imperceptibly until they spanned her rib cage.

"I'll get some candles," she said shakily. "This happens frequently, you see." She stepped away from him quickly. "I'll be right back."

"Oh, no. I'm afraid of the dark," he said. "I'm coming with you." He hooked a thumb into a belt loop on her side, which placed his fist at the swell of her hip. "Lead the way."

She felt her way around the shelves and racks, stumbling in the dark and ever aware of the figure looming close behind her, bumping into her every few steps.

"We have to turn right up the stairwell. It's rather tight."

"I'm right behind you," he said, and placed his other hand on the opposite side of her waist.

It took them several minutes to navigate the dark stairs, for in the narrow confines of the stairwell even the lightning flashes didn't provide them with any illumination.

"Here we are," she said with relief when they reached the second floor. She wasn't afraid of the darkness, or of the storm, or of being left without electricity. She was terrified of the sensations this man, and his touch, aroused in her. "Wait here. The candles are in the kitchen."

"Hurry," he said.

She laughed and tripped toward the drawer where she knew she would find a serviceable candle and matches. They were exactly where they should be, but she didn't seem to be capable of striking the match. Her hands were trembling and totally useless.

"Damn!" she cursed under her breath.

"What's the matter?" He spoke from directly behind her. She hadn't heard his approach and dropped the matchbox in surprise.

"Did I frighten you?" he asked solicitously.

"Yes."

"I'm sorry."

"That's all right. I can't seem to get the match struck."

It seemed imperative that some kind of light banish this darkness. It was too complete, too encapsulating, too intimate. His nearness was making her extremely nervous and edgy.

He took up the matchbox from where she had dropped it on the countertop. With one swipe across the bottom of the box the match flared to life.

"Thank you," she murmured as she lifted the candle toward the small flame. She looked up at him and found his face unnecessarily close to hers.

"You're welcome," he answered. He leaned down slightly and she was held in breathless suspension when she thought he was about to kiss her. Instead, he blew softly on the match and it went out, the smoke wafting between their faces.

Was it relief or disappointment she felt? Hurriedly she turned away from him and moved toward the door that connected the tiny kitchen to the living room.

"I have other candles in here," she said by way of explanation. Quickly, with the candle providing a small circle of light, she traversed the living room, stopping periodically to ignite a scented candle. Soon the room was bathed in a soft, fragrant glow.

"When you said you had some candles, you meant it," he teased from the door of the kitchen when a dozen or more candles had been lit.

"They're really for aesthetic purposes, but as you can see, sometimes they're functional as well."

She stood awkwardly, bare feet chastely together, hands self-consciously clasped in front of her. What now? "Would you like some coffee?" she asked.

"The electricity?"

"I have a gas stove."

"Great. That sounds good."

She walked toward him, taking one of the larger candles in its brass holder with her. He moved aside and she brushed past him into the kitchen.

"Don't feel like you have to entertain me," he said as she filled a percolator with water, "but I don't relish roaming around that maze out there without even the benefit of streetlights."

She smiled over her shoulder as she spooned coffee into the metal basket. "What kind of American would I be to deny aid and comfort to a fellow countryman? Where are you from, Reeves?" Reeves? Not Mr. Grant?

"I grew up in California. Went to UCLA. Started working professionally as a photographer during college." She had lit the stove and placed the percolator on the burner. "Say, listen, would I be presuming too much if I changed clothes? I'm still rather soggy."

"Yes . . . I mean no! By all means. You must be uncomfortable."

"I'll go down and change in the bookstore—"

"No. Use the bathroom. Here, take a candle down to get your bags."

She hurried past him and got another candle from the living room.

"Thanks," he said as he took it from her and loped down the stairs. He had certainly gained confidence since he had stumbled up behind her only moments before, clinging to her as if his life depended on it. He was back within a minute and she directed him through her bedroom to the bathroom, hoping that it was halfway presentable. She knew there was at least one damp towel lying on the floor. When one lived alone, one didn't give more than rudimentary attention to orderliness.

By the time the coffee was done he was back, wearing another pair of jeans, another casual shirt—this one soft yellow—and socks. No shoes.

"The coffee smells good," he said from the door.

"Have a seat. I'll bring it in there. This kitchen is barely large enough for one person."

He was sprawled on the sofa, ensconced in the deep cushions of one corner, when she came in carrying the tray with the coffee, cream, sugar, and two spoons, cups, and saucers.

She set the tray on the low table in front of the couch. Actually, it was two ceramic elephants with a piece of glass suspended between them. She poured the steaming, aromatic coffee into one cup and asked, "Anything in it?"

"No. I've learned to do without luxuries in some of the places I've been, so I've grown accustomed to drinking whatever is available." He sipped the scalding liquid. "Unless my sense of taste fails me, this is American coffee."

She laughed. "I have my parents send it over every few months."

"Ah, delicious." He smacked his lips.

She poured her own coffee and settled into the opposite corner of the sofa. His long legs were stretched out in front of him. In contrast, she tucked her feet under her legs.

"What else do you miss from home?" His question was casual—almost too casual. Did it portend more than surface curiosity?

"Conveniences. Fast-food restaurants. My soap opera." He laughed. "Not much else. I miss my parents, though they came over last year to visit. Lucerne is a charming place. The Swiss are an intelligent, industrious, and gracious people. I've traveled extensively in Europe. One day I aspire to write about it. You're rarely in the States, Reeves. What do you miss?"

Not a woman, she thought as he began to rattle off inconsequential things. He would never be without a woman. In the soft flickering firelight of the candles his hair took on an auburn cast as it tumbled riotously around his head. Just under his eyes, sprinkling his cheekbones, was a collection of freckles, which had been washed out by the harsh fluorescent lighting in the bookshop.

Taken apart, his features weren't classically handsome. His nose was a bit too slender. His mouth was almost too wide. The chin was a little too stubborn. But his eyes were fabulously green and well fringed by thick, spiky lashes. All put together, he was rakishly attractive. His virility was threatening—a threat no woman could resist.

He wore his clothes negligently. The fresh shirt he hadn't bothered to button even as much as the one he had taken off, and the curling mat of hair revealed beneath its folds was most appealing.

Jordan realized that he had stopped talking. "More coffee?" she asked, trying to draw enough air in her lungs to articulate the offer.

"No thank you."

Another silence descended. He stared at her from a distance the width of one cushion of the sofa. Unintentionally, but quite automatically, he reached across the cushion and captured her hand, which lay on her thigh. She didn't take it away.

The candles cast gigantic shadows against the walls of

the cozy room. The eggshell-white plaster had been chiseled off one wall, baring the ancient bricks behind it and adding character to the room. Tasteful graphics advertising concerts, ballets, and art shows had been sealed in thin brass frames and mounted on the walls.

The tall, wide windows of one wall were draped in a paisley print in tones of gold and brown. The fabric was repeated on the sofa and on the pillows tossed into one brown club chair. The hardwood floor, which shone with a patina only age can provide, was unrelieved by rugs that would have detracted from its beauty.

"I like your apartment." His thumb rotated hypnotically over her wrist, then slipped lower to explore the center of her palm. He wasn't looking at her apartment. He was looking at her mouth.

"Thank you," she said thickly. "I . . . decorated it myself. I re-covered the cushions of the couch."

"They're lovely," he replied, but his eyes were on her breasts, not the sofa. She swallowed convulsively as his eyes journeyed back up to her face and met her misty gray stare. Never in his life had Reeves been so captivated by a pair of eyes. Their light gray color was unusual, but their uniqueness was compounded by the dark blue ring that encircled that intriguing iris. The rarity of them, however, went beyond their mere physical aspects. They possessed a life and spirit all their own. The blue band surrounding that clear gray iris seemed to narrow and widen at will, allowing only fleeting glimpses into the soul of the woman. It became tantamount to Reeves Grant's well-being to see and know all the secrets those bewitching eyes harbored.

He stared into them now and saw himself reflected in

their depths. He longed to be there in actuality, inside her head, knowing what she was thinking. He moved closer to her.

Jordan's heart was pounding so hard she thought surely he could hear it or see it as it stirred the fabric stretched over her now taut breasts. His eyes were too compelling, his body too warm, his hand too hot as it continued to caress hers.

Fighting the impulse to move toward him, she pulled at her hand in an attempt to release it. He didn't surrender it easily. She tugged on it more firmly and said, "I'll put this away if you don't want anymore." Her hand was relinquished as she stood and picked up the tray. Her trembling fingers could barely maintain their grasp of it.

"I guess I'd better try the telephone again," he said without enthusiasm.

She was coming back into the living room after setting the tray on the kitchen table when he replaced the receiver on the cradle of the extension phone. Raising imploring eyes to her, he said, "It's still dead."

A thunderbolt punctuated the announcement.

2

~oooooooooooo~

Why don't you stay here?" The words were out before she could debate the wisdom of speaking them. She knew that was what he wanted her to say. At that moment the consequences weren't considered. The obvious risks didn't matter. It was the right thing to say in that given situation.

"I thought you'd never ask." He smiled broadly.

Lest he jump to the wrong conclusion about her spontaneous invitation, she said quickly, "You can have the bedroom. I'll sleep out here on the sofa."

"I wouldn't hear of it," he said, bowing gallantly. "By

all means, the lady should keep her bed. I'll take the sofa."

"You won't even fit on it," she objected.

"If you could see some of the places I've slept when on assignment, you'd realize how great this sofa looks."

"Well, if you're sure . . ."

"I am."

"Okay. You may take a turn in the bathroom while I make up the couch for you."

"Right." He saluted her and, lifting one of the bags he had carried upstairs with him earlier, went into the bathroom. He came back almost immediately and picked up a candle. Grinning sardonically, he returned to the bathroom.

Jordan hastily retrieved extra blankets and sheets from her bedroom closet and smiled when she heard him humming over splashing water.

With dispatch, she made the couch into a facsimile of a comfortable bed. She plumped the pillow and slipped a fresh case over it. She was straightening the blanket one more time when she heard him come in behind her.

"Brushing one's teeth by candlelight is an incredibly sexy experience," he drawled.

He was still dressed, but the collar of his shirt was damp where he had washed. Judiciously she ignored his leading remark. "Do you need anything else?" she asked softly.

He set his bag at his feet and took three steps forward until he was standing inches from her. "No. Till my dying day, I'll appreciate your hospitality, my little American cousin."

Before she realized what was happening, his hands were on her shoulders and he was leaning down to kiss her. His lips met hers firmly in a smacking, friendly, closed-mouth kiss. No harm done, she thought analytically.

But when he should have withdrawn, he didn't. His hands remained on her shoulders—indeed, his fingers were moving in a near caress. His lips hovered over hers. His breath mingled with hers, found the blend delightful, and joyously united with it into an invisible vapor that ghosted between their mouths.

Taking her stunned immobility as an invitation, his lips hesitantly brushed across hers once, twice, then came to rest against the soft flesh. The pressure of his mouth increased until it could be said that he was truly kissing her. How easy it would be to accept this kiss, to lean against his strength, to be penetrated by the heat that emanated from his body.

But the sheer encompassing quality of his embrace frightened Jordan. The totality of her loss of will alarmed her. If she surrendered, it would be an absolute capitulation, and she couldn't chance that. Her hands went to his shoulders and pushed against them halfheartedly, but he accepted the discouragement and stepped away from her.

"Good night," he murmured as his eyes bore into hers.

"Good night," she answered, picking up a candle and scurrying toward the bedroom. She collapsed against the closed door and drew several restorative breaths. When she felt more normal and her pulse was beating at a comfortable tempo again, she went into the bathroom.

She creamed her face, brushed her teeth, and took down her hair. All of these routine things she did automatically, her mind in a turmoil, her thoughts traitorous to the decision she had made moments before. What were his lips capable of when his passion was unleashed? The hands that had caressed her shoulders only hinted at their talent to heighten the senses.

Foolishness! she chided herself as she took the candle into her bedroom. He was only being polite. It was a kiss of gratitude. Friendship. Comrades abroad. Nothing more.

She set the candle on the bedside table and turned down the quilted spread and colorful sheets. Her fingers were working with the snap of her slacks when the door behind her swung open on silent hinges.

Only the light from one candle on the coffee table was behind him, but she could see that he wore only a pair of pajama bottoms, which rode low on his hips. His frame completely filled the doorway, his arms spread wide, his hands bracing him on each side of the jamb.

She stared at him with a mixture of fear and excitement. One hand went to her throat to capture her heart, which had leaped there. The other settled over her stomach, trying vainly to still the disquieting flutter. She felt helpless, caught up in something from which there was no escape. Escape? Did she want to escape?

"Are you going to scream?" he asked quietly. He began to move toward her.

"I don't know," she answered honestly, shaking her head in desperation.

He stood only a few feet from her now. The magnificent proportions of his physique were revealed to her clearly and she admitted that she had never seen a man who stirred her feminine instincts as did this man.

"I don't think so," she whispered. Then his hands came up to cup her face and tilt it back for his kiss. Her eyes were already closing as she said, "No, I'm not going to scream."

This time there was no hesitancy. His lips claimed hers in a fierce kiss. Then his mouth opened and left no room for argument on that claim. He possessed her mouth thoroughly, and without resistance she parted her lips and honored his ownership.

His tongue rubbed sensuously against hers and then went deeper to explore the mysteries of her mouth. He solved each one in turn. His arms wrapped around her. Smoothing over her back, his hands settled on her waist and drew her closer until their bodies melded together. Teasingly, his mouth moved over hers, elusively avoiding her lips, which pursued it. When a small, frustrated moan escaped her, he rewarded her tenacity by taking her mouth under his once again.

Her arms came up and locked behind his neck. Without separating, they fell to the bed and lay on the pillows, which welcomed them as if they belonged.

He raised his head and gazed down at her with fevered eyes. He spoke rapidly, as though he had been saving up things to say, and now that the opportunity had presented itself, he didn't want to lose it. "Your hair is beautiful. So dark and shiny." His fingers sifted through the silky strands. "Your complexion doesn't need make-up. Your eyes . . . God, you're gorgeous, Jordan. Kiss me again. Please."

She needed no coaxing. Her hands tangled in the

coarse auburn hair and pulled his face down to hers. Their mouths met with equal need, each hot and moist and seeking appeasement for a newborn thirst that seemed unquenchable.

He forsook the wellspring of her mouth to plant kisses along her cheek and ear. He tasted the lobe with a velvet-rough tongue. Jordan's fingertips explored the hard, bunched muscles of his shoulders as capricious lips skipped along her neck. With precision, his hand moved between their bodies and covered her breast. An inquisitive thumb stroked across the crest, which impertinently demanded attention.

"Reeves," she groaned, and arched upward against him. Suddenly she realized what she was doing. Not until an hour ago had she ever seen this man. Now she was in bed with him, allowing him—no, *begging* him—to kiss her and caress her with matchless intimacy. This was not trivial kissing. This was making love. With a stranger! Was she mad? She must stop this. Now.

But his hands had slipped under her sweater and were learning the lush curves of her breasts. "Reeves, please . . . no," she pleaded. "No . . . I can't. I don't . . ."

"I do, Jordan. I do. But not like this. Never before like this."

Then the sweater was being peeled over her head and she lay exposed to his ardent eyes. "My God," he breathed as his heated gaze devoured her. Tenderly, his hands caressed her and he watched in adoring wonder as her breasts responded readily, eagerly, to the manipulation of his fingertips.

Embarrassed by his scrutiny and her response to his touch, she shut her eyes. His mouth closed over her breast. The nipple knew the sweet nudging of his tongue.

He tugged on her gently, yet she felt it deep within her body, igniting a fuse that raced through her veins, leaving behind a thrilling conflagration. She cried his name softly.

He lifted his head and asked anxiously, "Did I hurt you?"

"No, no," she sobbed, and clasped his head, drawing it back to her.

"Jordan," he murmured against her dewy skin. "You're delicious." His mouth continued to torture and tease and she knew that she was lost. The battle was over before it was begun. He was the victor because he really had no opponent. She had forfeited. She wanted this now as much as he did.

When he undid her slacks and slipped them and her panties down her legs, she made no move to resist. He stood, and with a quick yank to the string at his waist the pajamas slid down his legs to the floor. He lay down again and gathered her to him.

His body moved along hers, detailing the physical differences between them. His leg with its hair-roughened skin lay across hers, heavy and protective. His chest raked against her breasts, tickling them with the crinkly brush that covered it. A thumb feathered her cheek as he kissed her long and deep.

His hand smoothed over the satin skin of her hip and along her thighs, between them. His sharp intake of breath echoed hers when he touched the gate of her femininity. He found it pliant and ready for his caress. He stroked her appreciatively. "Jordan, you feel so good. So incredibly good."

His fingers worked like a magic wand that showered her body with iridescent sparks of ecstasy. Fervent kisses were rained on her breasts. His body continued to stroke hers. With every movement, every soft panting breath, she beseeched him to explore further.

When she could bear no more, she clutched him tightly. He moved over her, but restrained himself long enough to ask hoarsely, "Jordan, is there any reason why I shouldn't do this?"

Yes! There were a hundred reasons. Thousands. A vision of another face was projected onto her brain, but she refused to look at it. She was at such a level of desire that nothing else mattered. Reeves had kissed her, caressed her like no other man ever had. She couldn't deny the sleeping passion he had awakened. None of this should be happening. But it was. And she wanted it to happen.

She shook her head against the pillow. "No, no reason."

He fused their bodies together so consummately that she gasped her pleasure in the form of his name. "Yes, Jordan, yes," he rasped against her ear. "It's good. Wonderful."

The rightness of it didn't escape their passion-clouded minds. Each recognized the harmonious way their bodies coupled. The rhythm with which they moved seemed rehearsed. They withheld nothing. Barriers didn't exist. Inhibitions were banished.

Nor did they hasten.

Every move was calculated to bring the other pleasure. Each caress was slow and provocative, its sole intention to please. They each became drugged with the essense of the other until the culmination exploded upon them. It rocketed through them simultaneously. Reeves buried his face deep within the curve of her shoulder. Jordan clasped him to her and gloried in the fulfillment.

"I don't understand this." She shifted closer to him and rested her cheek on the dark hair on his chest.

"What's to understand?" he asked softly. His arm cradled her against him while the other hand stroked her hair.

"This isn't like me. I've never . . . I haven't been with a man since my husband," she admitted abashedly. He probably wouldn't believe her. She hardly believed it herself.

He lifted his head off the pillow and gazed down at her face, which was shadowed by the single candle on the bedside table. His index finger traced down her cheek, still flushed with his love. "You don't have to justify that or apologize for it. I think I would have known it anyway."

She raised her eyes and looked at him. "Was I that awkward?" she asked.

"You were perfect." He kissed her gently on the lips. "But physically it didn't *feel* like you were often with a man."

She dipped her face again into the shelter of his shoulder and he chuckled softly at her embarrassment. They lay silent and pensive for long moments, content to enjoy the warmth, the touch, the scent, the nearness of the other. His voice was low and confidence-inspiring when he said, "Tell me about your husband."

Her hand, which had been idly charting his ribs, came to rest. "We married after I graduated from college. We were married for four years. He was killed in a car crash."

"I'm sorry. It must have been a terrible time for you."

She sighed. "We were separated at the time he was killed, Reeves. Charles was a salesman—an unsuccessful one. He went from job to job, chasing rainbows, never thinking realistically. I traipsed after him for years, from city to city, from state to state, always hoping that I'd be able to hang up curtains before he came home and told me of his latest prospect that would require moving again.

"I finally got tired of the transient lifestyle and left him. I got a job with a newspaper writing society page articles. It wasn't a very exciting life, but it was stable. Charles kept begging me to come back to him, but I refused to unless he promised to settle down. He was killed several months later."

Reeves breathed heavily and drew her closer. "I hope you don't harbor any guilt feelings over leaving him."

She laughed drily. "I probably would have, but after his death his girl friend came to see me and guiltily confessed all the lurid details. They had been lovers long before I moved out."

"Sounds like he was a real winner," Reeves said sarcastically.

"Don't be too hard on Charles. He couldn't help the way he was any more than any of us can."

"I think you're being magnanimous," he whispered. He cupped her chin in his fist and raised her face to receive a soft kiss.

He practically threw her from him and sat bolt upright when the lights suddenly flashed on. When both realized what had happened, they burst out laughing.

"I've lived through wars, famines, and floods, and I nearly have a heart attack when the electricity comes back on." He was raking his hands through his hair in a most endearing, boyish way.

"What time is it?" she asked.

He checked his wristwatch. "Just after two."

"Well, the power has been restored in almost record time," she commented with a laugh.

"Stay where you are, woman. I'll go around and turn off all the lights."

"Like that?" she asked. She sat up and stared at him in astonishment as he stepped over the discarded pajama bottoms.

His brows lowered over lascivious eyes as they treated themselves to a leisurely perusal of her breasts. "Do you object?" he taunted.

She smiled mischievously. "Not if you hurry back."

"Insatiable wench," he teased as he strode out of the room.

Jordan fell back against the pillows, raising her arms high above her head and stretching luxuriously. She sighed in deep contentment. A silly smile curled her lips as her eyes strayed over the room, which seemed to have changed character with the presence of Reeves Grant.

Her eyes lit briefly on the Lalique perfume bottles on her dresser. They passed the collection, but then came back to look at it more closely. Helmut. Helmut had given her the crystal last week for a "no occasion" present.

For an instant, when Reeves had asked her if there were any reason why he should not complete the act of loving, Helmut's face had flickered through her mind. Her being with Reeves tonight wasn't fair to Helmut at all. How would she handle that?

Should she tell Reeves about Helmut? It really was

none of his concern, but it might be better to get everything out in the open at the outset. The outset of what? She had no reason to believe that this would go any further than the present. Perhaps it would be better to keep her counsel until Reeves indicated what his intentions were.

No, she wouldn't tell him anything just now.

But when Reeves came back into the room and switched off the light, she knew she wanted to be honest with him.

"Reeves," she said as he slid in beside her and took her in his arms. "Reeves—"

"They're all out. Should we just let this one last candle burn down? I don't want *all* the lights to be off or I can't see you." His voice was husky as his lips sought the base of her throat and the vulnerable triangle there.

"Reeves . . ."

"Hm?"

"I want to . . . ah . . . Reeves, please . . . talk . . ."

His hand splayed over the smooth expanse of her stomach while his lips fluttered across her breasts, bringing her nipples alert with longing. "Do you really want to talk? Now?" he asked a second before his mouth settled over hers. The intrusion of his tongue prevented her from speaking, but it made no difference. She had forgotten what she was going to say anyway.

Helmut Eckherdt proffered his hand to Reeves Grant and exclaimed, "Mr. Grant, I've barely seen you since your arrival. I hope you have accommodated yourself with food and drink." His smile was startling in his handsome face, and he was totally unaware of the tension between the photographer and Jordan.

"Thank you, Mr. Eckherdt. I've been enjoying myself immensely. More so each minute." Reeves's eyes slid over to Jordan, who was standing stoic and pale beside Helmut.

"Oh, excuse me, darling," Helmut apologized, and tucked her arm under his. "Mr. Reeves Grant, may I present Mrs. Jordan Hadlock. She is a citizen of your country, but not for long, I hope."

Helmut smiled adoringly down into Jordan's tight white face as she offered her hand for Reeves to shake. He didn't take her hand immediately. He paused momentarily. The blood rushed to her head and she felt dizzy. Her mouth went dry. Surely he wouldn't say anything about last night! He wouldn't be that callous. Slowly, his hand came up and reached for hers. His fingers wrapped around hers tightly and he shook her hand.

"A pleasure, Mrs. Hadlock," he said silkily.

"Thank you," she murmured.

"You will be seeing a lot of Reeves—may I call you Reeves?—for the next several days, my dear," Helmut said. "He is doing a feature on me for an American magazine. He is a photojournalist."

"I'm familiar with Mr. Grant's work," Jordan said quietly. She bravely raised her eyes to meet the bold green ones glaring at her. "I saw your piece on the IRA in *Time*. It was comprehensive and interesting. You handled a very delicate subject realistically but with compassion."

"Thank you, Mrs. Hadlock. I thought that this time I'd work on a less depressing topic. I was most eager to meet Mr. Eckherdt. I think the American public will love an article about one of the world's most affluent men."

"I would like for Jordan to be included in the article,

Reeves. As a matter of fact, you may want to get your camera ready. In a few minutes I'll be making public our engagement."

Jordan whirled to face him. "Helmut!" she cried. "Why . . . why didn't you tell me?"

"Because I wanted it to be a surprise." His teeth flashed whitely in a dazzling smile. "And if I had told you, you would have thought up another excuse to postpone the inevitable. You *will* become Mrs. Eckherdt, my darling. It's only a matter of time. Have you or have you not consented to marry me?"

On a recent excursion to Zermatt, she had wearily consented to *think* about marrying him after hours of his playful badgering. She had planned to broach the subject at a later time and reasonably explain to him that she wasn't ready to marry again. But the time had never been right and now he was going to make official their tentative engagement with an announcement. And Reeves! God, could this be happening?

The beautiful gown, which Helmut had insisted on buying her for this reception, was suddenly constricting. The room was too crowded. The champagne she had drunk seemed to be boiling in her stomach and threatening to come back up. Her head was pounding. And all the while Reeves was standing close and staring at her malevolently.

Jordan felt detached from the scene as she watched Helmut call everyone's attention to them. Gradually, conversations were hushed, heads were turned, plates of sumptuous food were set aside, as the guests politely turned toward their host.

"I'm sure that most of you have met Jordan by now. It is with pleasure I tell you tonight that she is soon to become my wife." A rumble of reaction rolled toward them. The women looked at her with envy, the men with appreciation; some, selfishly more concerned with their own private love affairs, seemed only blandly interested.

Jordan recoiled from their staring eyes. Trancelike, she obliged him when Helmut pulled her into his arms and kissed her chastely on the lips. She was aware of a camera flashing on them. Reeves was taking pictures of her kissing another man.

Helmut was speaking again. "To seal our engagement, I want to present Jordan with this ring." From his pocket he extracted a velvet ring box and flipped it open. He took out a platinum ring on which was mounted the largest, most tastelessly ostentatious emerald-cut diamond Jordan had ever seen. He picked up her clammy, limp left hand and slid the ring on her third finger. It felt as heavy as a ball and chain. She looked up at him and smiled sickly. The camera flashed repeatedly.

She wanted to turn on Reeves and scream at him to stop. This wasn't real. None of this mattered or had any bearing on what had happened last night, but the flash on the camera was persistent. The crowd undulated toward her to extend their congratulations and view the diamond on her hand.

Reeves watched as Jordan frantically caught at Helmut's sleeve. The blood thundered through his veins. He was barely able to restrain himself from grabbing Jordan and shaking her until she begged him to stop. When she was thoroughly contrite and pleading for merciful forgiveness, he wanted to kiss her until she knew without a doubt that she belonged to him. But she didn't. She was leaning against Helmut with feminine helplessness. Never in his life had Reeves known such jealousy or anger.

He saw Helmut duck his head and place his ear near her mouth. Her lips barely moved against Helmut's flesh, but Reeves remembered just how that felt. She whispered something to Helmut and then Reeves read the man's lips as he answered, "Of course, my darling."

Reeves had put his hand in his pocket to find another lens, but his hand had closed around one of the filters his camera often required. When he saw Helmut press his mouth against Jordan's slightly parted lips, his fingers clenched reflexively. He was impervious to the breaking glass that sliced through three of his fingers.

It wasn't until he withdrew his hand and saw the blood dripping from it that he hastened to grab a napkin off the buffet table to stanch the flow. Helmut was making another announcement, obviously at the request of his fiancée.

"Ladies and gentlemen, Jordan has asked, since you are all friends and there are no members of the press here tonight, that you refrain from notifying them of our upcoming marriage. Understandably, she doesn't want it to be publicized until she can contact her parents in the United States."

Reeves let the crowd stream around him as they exclaimed over the fairy-tale couple. He watched Jordan as she graciously received well-wishes. When a large, buxom, overjeweled matron drew her into a suffocating embrace, he met her eyes over the woman's massive shoulders.

Damn her! Those blue-ringed gray eyes looked at him pleadingly. They were wide and apprehensive, compelling, and totally arresting. How dare she make a prize fool out of him and then look at him like that! He didn't allow his frigid stare to warm. But his indifference was all for show. Even now he didn't know which he would rather do, slap her hard across her lying mouth or fling her to the floor and make love to her with the wild hunger that made the pressure in his loins almost unbearable.

Jordan sank weakly onto a satin Louis XIV chair. She stared absently at the priceless marble floor under her silver sandal. One of the thin straps had cut a deep red groove into her little toe. She longed to ease off the shoe and walk around in her bare feet as she had done last night. Last night.

She directed her gaze across the floor to where maids and waiters were gathering up the refuse of the party. One was mopping up spilled champagne, while another was emptying ashes from crystal ashtrays into a copper butler's helper. Subordinates were loading trays with empty plates and napkins.

Reeves and Helmut were standing near the buffet table chatting congenially. Reeves tossed a handful of peanuts into his mouth and then threw back his head and laughed uproariously at something Helmut had said.

How had she, Jordan Hadlock, managed to get herself into such an untenable predicament? If only she had asked Reeves what project had brought him to Lucerne. Wasn't that a logical question? If only he had mentioned that he was working on a feature story about a Swiss entrepreneur. Why hadn't the subject of his work come up? If only . . . If only . . .

What would have happened last night had Reeves known she was more or less "involved" with Helmut Eckherdt? Would that have mattered to him?

Helmut was at least a decade older than Reeves, was much wealthier, and commanded attention in an intimidating fashion. Yet, as Jordan observed the two men now, she saw that Reeves met Helmut as an equal. He wasn't cowed by Helmut's wealth or the power the industrialist wielded.

Both men were handsome. Helmut had the classic blond coloring that could have graced an Alpine travel poster. His body was hard and strong, due to the hours he spent in his exercise room and with his personal masseur.

Reeves's body appeared to be naturally vital, requiring no maintenance. Each movement was graceful, casual, but indicative of subliminal power. He was blatantly American. His rugged good looks typified the pioneers of his heritage.

Jordan admired each of his gestures, thrilled to the rumbling sound of his laugh, the soft drawl of his voice. With a tenderness born of recollection, she watched his hands place the camera into its protective case, snap it shut, and then reach out to shake Helmut's hand. The fingers of one hand, she noticed, were wrapped in a napkin. Were there blood stains on it?

Last night those capable hands had caressed her until she writhed under their transporting touch. They had been sensitive to her responses, unhurried in caresses that brought her the most pleasure. His lips had followed suit, roving her body avariciously. His greed had been gratified.

The love words he had whispered in her ear had been as thrilling as his lovemaking. Charles, her husband, had been a silent lover. Never would she have guessed that those precious, disjointed phrases could convey such meaningful messages to her body and spirit.

Last night his words had been full of praise. What was

he thinking of her now as he and Helmut came toward her? She blinked back the tears that threatened at the corners of her eyes and tried to smile, but wasn't sure it looked like more than an aborted effort.

"My dear, I'm sorry to have kept you waiting so long," Helmut said. "I have some important matters that need to be seen to before business hours tomorrow. Reeves has offered to see you home in the launch and escort you to your door."

3

~eeooooooooo~

Jordan's eyes flew to Reeves, then just as quickly back to Helmut. "That isn't necessary. I can see myself home once we dock at the quay."

"Absolutely not, Mrs. Hadlock," Reeves said smoothly. "I've promised Helmut not to let you out of my sight until you are safely inside your front door."

Jordan had a strong urge to slap him. He was deliberately mocking her. While Helmut was gathering up her wrap and evening purse from the cloak room, Reeves was leaning negligently against a marble column, raking her up and down with insolent eyes.

"Ready, Jordan?" Helmut asked politely.

"Yes."

Helmut insisted on walking with them out the back of the château. Helmut's estate was situated on a private island several acres large in the Lake of Lucerne. The house, if it could be so humbly termed, was white painted brick trimmed with dark brown woodwork and shutters. Despite its modest architecture, it was a showplace. The interior was splendid. The grounds were a study of horticultural perfection.

He led Jordan and Reeves through the sculptured garden and down the stone steps to his private dock. A uniformed boatman helped them aboard a sleek craft after Helmut had kissed her good night. Helmut often hired motor taxis for an evening to shuttle his guests from his island in the lake to the shore. They were not luxurious launches, nor were they mediocre.

When she and Reeves were settled into deck chairs, the pilot started the inboard motor and they chugged away from the dock. Helmut waved them off until they disappeared into the darkness, the fine spray rising in their wake.

Jordan sat tensely in the low canvas chair, shivering slightly in the cold evening air. She snuggled deeper into her satin floor-length cape. She kept her eyes away from the man in the chair next to hers. The helmsman had his back to them as he navigated the smooth water, so they were all but alone.

Out of the darkness, she heard a scratching sound, then saw the flare of a match as it was put to the end of a cigarette. Reeves fanned out the match and conscientiously placed it in a pail of sand anchored to the glossy deck. Jordan caught the pungent aroma of the tobacco smoke as Reeves inhaled deeply on the cigarette and then exhaled slowly.

"I didn't know you smoked," she remarked quietly.

There was a long pause and she thought that either he hadn't heard her or that he planned to ignore her. Finally he said, "I don't. I quit years ago. I just started again."

"Oh."

He shifted around in his chair until he was facing her. He stared hard at her with cold green eyes as he drew once more on the cigarette, coughed, cursed the cough, and flicked the cigarette through the air to die a sudden, hissing death in the lake. "Is that all you can say? 'Oh'?"

"Reeves, please, I—"

"Spare me the theatrical explanations," he cut in sharply. "None is necessary, I assure you. We shared a great roll in the hay during a thunderstorm. Very romantic. Very cozy. I enjoyed it. You enjoyed it. That's all there was to it." He sliced his hands through the air to emphasize that the subject was closed and she noticed again the napkin-wrapped fingers.

His words had pierced her to the core, but her attention was momentarily distracted by the bloodstained napkin. "What happened to your hand?" she asked.

"What?" His agitation was apparent. Every muscle in his body was pulled taut and strained against the restriction of his clothing. *"What?"* he repeated more heatedly, as though she hadn't responded in the way he thought she should have.

"What happened to your hand?"

He looked at her in angry bewilderment and then down at his hand as if seeing it for the first time. "Oh, I . . . uh . . . cut it. It's fine."

"It's bleeding."

"Not anymore."

"Are you sure? Maybe—"

"I said it's fine."

"Let me see—"

"Will you forget my damned hand!" he roared. He stood up and stuffed his hands into the pockets of his tuxedo trousers, walking to the rail of the boat and leaning against it. She could tell by the heaving of his shoulders that he was almost gasping for air. Up until now she hadn't realized the extent of his fury.

He stood at the rail a long time, thumping his fists against the polished wood, looking out over the water and staring at the lights of Lucerne while they loomed larger on the horizon as the boat drew closer to the city. Jordan stared at his back and remained quiet. She longed to tell him about her relationship with Helmut, but his frame of mind wasn't conducive to calm explanations. She'd let him vent his temper, then she would try to explain.

When he spun around and faced her, she jumped. "It's not that I have scruples about sleeping with another man's fiancée," he sneered. "It's just that you lied to me. I despise mendacity, Jordan."

"I didn't—"

"What would Helmut think if he knew about last night? Hm? Would your diamond have been just a tiny bit smaller? Or *does* he know? Maybe you accommodate him so well that he's willing to overlook your occasional indiscretions. Maybe he shares you with his friends."

"Shut up!" she shouted as she flew out of the chair and almost lost her balance as she stumbled across the windy deck. "It isn't like that. I was going to tell you about

Helmut this morning, but you had split, hadn't you? When I woke up and saw you were gone, I couldn't decide if you were an incredibly vivid dream or a nightmare. I had slept with a tender, sensitive man who turned out to be a cad who sneaked out at first light. A one-night stand? Is that what all the boys in the locker room refer to me as?"

Tears now blurred her eyes and she swiped at them angrily. She hadn't wanted him to know how devastated she had been when she awoke long after the sun was up to find him gone without a trace. Had the mattress not born the imprint of his body, had not the spicy fragrance of his cologne still clung to the linens, she might have thought he had been a figment.

But the most evident traces of his existence were on her body. Her lips were slightly bruised and chafed from the ardency of his kisses. Her breasts tingled with remembrances of his caresses. If she concentrated, she could accurately recall the sensation of having him full and deep inside her, imagine it still. No. He had been all too real.

"I came back this afternoon, but you had conveniently deserted the premises," he fired back at her. "Were you in there all the time while I knocked on your door like some frustrated Romeo?"

Yes, she had been. By midafternoon, ashamed and distraught over what had happened, she had closed the shop and gone upstairs to lie down. She hadn't slept much the night before. Helmut had called to tell her he would have one of his servants pick her up and escort her through the alleys of the old town to the quay, where a motor launch would be waiting for her. She was to bring her clothes for the reception with her and change at the château, where Helmut kept a suite available for her use.

She had only hung up the telephone when she heard the knocking on her door downstairs. Surreptitiously she peered through the closed shutters of her bedroom window down into the street. Her heart lurched when she saw the sun shining on Reeves's hair. He tried the locked door knob again a bit impatiently, then knocked harder. He even called her name and glanced up toward the window. She jumped back in time for him not to see her.

Why hadn't she gone down and opened the door? What had made her stand there, petrified of seeing him again? Shame? Embarrassment? Maybe in the light of day he wouldn't find her so attractive. Or maybe he wouldn't be nearly so appealing to her. She dashed that thought. He was the most attractive man she had ever seen, by candlelight or sunlight. What had kept her from going down and flinging the door open wide and throwing herself into his arms?

Fear.

For the past few years she had lived by her own devices, learning from her own mistakes, celebrating her own accomplishments. She had kept herself insulated from exterior intervention. She had once placed her life in a man's hands and it had ended disastrously. When she had finally left Charles, she had pledged never again to entrust her life to another human being. Charles's untimely death had irrevocably prevented her from returning to an unhappy marriage, but she had never again allowed herself to become attached to a man to the point of dependence.

For months Helmut had pursued her, but caution had

kept her from totally accepting his affection. That same caution had held her back from charging down the stairs that afternoon to embrace Reeves with all the happiness that welled up inside her at the mere sight of him.

My God! She had slept with this man. For the span of a brief few hours her life *had* been in his hands. All control, subconsciously, had been relinquished to him. If that weren't courting danger, she didn't know what was. So, as she stood there watching him take a note pad out of his pocket, scribble a hasty message, and slip it into her mail slot, she determined that she would never see him again.

After he left, she had raced down the stairs, retrieved the note, and held it in shaky fingers as she read:

Sweet (sweeter, sweetest) Jordan,
Forgive me for ducking out without saying goodbye, but you were sleeping so soundly I didn't have the heart to wake you. (Confession: I peeked under the blanket. Beautiful.) I wanted to check into a room (at the Europa, incidentally) and clean up before presenting myself at your door again. Unfortunately, you have ill-chosen this time to run an errand. I'll be busy the early part of the evening (business), but if you will keep a light burning, I'll be by later. (Memories of last night will keep *me* burning.) Until then . . .

Reeves

Her recent resolve not to see him again evaporated like smoke and vanished into the atmosphere. Somehow she would live through one of Helmut's "small, intimate cocktail parties" for a "few close friends." After a reasonable period of time, she would plead a headache and rush home to wait for Reeves. He would ask her if she'd been out. She would tell him about Helmut, but make it clear there was no commitment on her part. He would say that he was glad of that and that he understood. He would take her in his arms. Kiss her.

The best-laid plans of mice and men . . .

"Make it good, Jordan." His snarling words snapped her out of the past and into the present. Her dazed eyes focused on him. The wind was whipping his hair into a wild disarray that, combined with the feral gleam in his eyes, made him appear diabolical.

Obviously he thought she was contriving some story about her absence from the shop that afternoon. She answered truthfully. "Yes, I was there, Reeves." He seemed surprised by her answer and the harsh lines around his mouth softened, but slightly. "At the time, I didn't think we should see each other again."

"Oh, I agree," he said. "It can get sticky when one is marrying one of the world's richest men and takes a lover at the same time. People talk, you know."

"No!" She stamped her foot in frustration. "I didn't know that Helmut was going to announce our engagement tonight."

"But you were unofficially engaged?"

"No. Well, not exactly . . . he . . ."

"Yes?" he cooed, and folded his arms across his chest in an arrogant stance that was most irritating.

She licked her lips and tried to brush back the strands of hair that were whirling around her face. "Be reasonable, Reeves. Can't you see that I'm not a part of that?" she demanded, vaguely gesturing toward the château they had just left.

"But you will be soon. Quite an accomplishment for a shopkeeper from Iowa."

She ignored the sarcastic barb and went on. "Helmut came into my shop one day to buy a newspaper. We chatted. He was charming, flirtatious. I thought nothing of it. But that evening, just as I was closing, he came back in and invited me out for coffee."

"Did you know who he was?" he asked incisively.

"I thought I had seen . . ." she hedged. Then she looked up into the piercing eyes and knew it would be useless to lie, though he would take the truth in the wrong way. "Yes," she said. "I knew who he was."

"Uh-huh."

Some force stronger than her anger kept her from slapping that knowing smirk off his mouth. She swallowed her rage and continued levelly. "For several consecutive days he came into the shop and we talked. Then he invited me to dinner. I went. We began to see each other more often until . . ."

When she wavered, he pressed her, "Go on, Jordan, I'm fascinated."

"He began to court me—presents, flowers, expensive trinkets that I neither wanted nor required."

He leered at her wickedly. "And what did Helmut get in return for these 'expensive trinkets'?"

"Nothing!" she exclaimed. Just then the boat bumped against the pilings of the quay and she was hurled at him.

His strong arms caught her and pulled her against his chest. The hold wasn't tender as it had been the night before. His hands were like steel talons on her upper arms and the face that lowered to hers was ugly with disgust. "Do you really think that I'm dense enough to believe that a man as rich and urbane as Helmut

Eckherdt hasn't taken advantage of this?" He thrust himself at her in a manner that left no doubt of his meaning. The implication was insulting and humiliating.

She squirmed and pushed against him. "Let me go," she said through clenched teeth. "Don't touch me again."

The boatman approached them meekly and Reeves slowly disengaged his hands from her arms. She pivoted away, avoiding the boatman's curious eyes as she picked up her purse. Out of the corner of her eye she saw Reeves sling his camera case over his shoulder.

As soon as she was helped to the quay by the boat's pilot, Reeves leaped beside her and grabbed her arm again.

"I told you not to touch me," she said, and tried to jerk her arm free. She could have spared herself the effort. Her strength was no match for his.

"No. I promised Helmut I'd see you to your door, and I never lie." The veiled accusation wasn't lost on her and she had a stinging rejoinder forming in her mind when he asked abruptly, "How in the hell do we get to your bookshop from here?"

He was determined to see her home. The best course of action was to go along with him. She nodded in the general direction and said, "Turn left at the second street."

They walked in silence for several blocks as the streets soon narrowed and became the mazelike alleys where only foot traffic was permitted. Jordan stumbled behind his long, unfaltering strides. Her feet ached abominably, but she'd be damned before she would complain or ask him to slow down.

With relief she saw her shop as they came around the

last corner. When they reached the door, Reeves let the strap of his camera case slide down his arm until the bag plopped to the ground. Before she could react, he had nailed her to the stone wall with the pressure of his own body. Her hands were held on either side of her face by his firm grip on her wrists.

"I have to hand it to you, Jordan. You're quite an actress. Maybe you missed your calling." His voice was deceptively soft, his breath warm and gently caressing against her cold cheeks. "Those wide gray eyes full of almost virginal timidity. Those sincere declarations that I'd been the only man since—" He broke off abruptly on a bitter note. He threw back his head and squeezed his eyes shut in an agonized expression. "God, what a fool I was," he laughed mirthlessly.

Then his eyes were hard on her again. His face lowered until only a breath separated them. "I fell for your act hook, line, and sinker." His eyes roamed over her face, taking in each feature, studying it. "And you're still playing your charade," he said huskily. "It's really quite touching. The shine of tears in those damn gray eyes. The innocent expression. The trembling lips."

The last words were lost as his mouth descended on hers and moved over it bruisingly. It was a blistering kiss, meant to hurt and debase. But when he felt no resistance, his plundering became persuasion. After only a heartbeat of hesitation, she parted her lips and welcomed the invasion of his tongue. Her wrists were suddenly released from their traps, but she only used that freedom to wrap her hands around his neck and delight in the feel of the hair that lay outside his collar.

He parted her cape and agilely slipped one hand inside. It caressed her waist, squeezing it slightly, appreciating its trim line. Then he moved closer, fitting his body to hers, aligning them in such a way that Jordan responded with a sensual adjustment of her own that took his breath.

Desire curled through her when she felt the strength of his virility through their clothes. Her tongue darted past his lips on a foray of its own. All the ugly accusations he had wrongly thrown at her melted under the heat of his kiss.

His hand stroked its way over her ribs and up to the curve of her breast. He kneaded it gently as his thumb lazily circled the rigid nipple under the silky fabric. He continued this heavenly torment as his lips pressed hot kisses into the curve of her shoulder left bare by her gown. His lips nibbled their way down her arm, pressed a kiss in the bend of her elbow, and then lifted her palm to receive a tribute from his mouth.

She reclined against the wall and sighed, touching his hair affectionately. Smiling up at him slumbrously, she watched him as he turned her hand over. He looked at the diamond ring.

In a voice as hard and cold as the jewel he said, "You see, Jordan. The only thing that separates you from the girls who sell their wares on street corners is the price you demand."

It took a moment for the words to sink in. They were so out of context with the soft caresses and the soothing voice that their meaning eluded her. When it registered with her passion-fogged mind, she thought the pain in her chest would surely kill her. She would die with his scathing insult as her eulogy.

But the cold reality of what he had said jolted her out of her lethargy like an icy bath. He was still holding her left hand as he smiled down at her smugly. Her right hand arced and met his cheek in a resounding slap.

For a moment he was stunned. There was no reaction. Then the fury filled his face with such terrible intent that Jordan thought he might very well murder her. Instead, he flung himself away.

Without a backward glance or another word, he hoisted the camera case over his shoulder and stalked away into the night shadows.

"English newsstand," Jordan answered the telephone the next day at midmorning.

"Hello, darling," Helmut said with his smooth, cultured voice. "How are you this morning? Did you enjoy the party held in your honor last night?"

"Hello, Helmut," she said. "I can only talk for a minute. I have some customers. Yes, I enjoyed the party very much. I only wish we had had time to discuss—"

"I know what you're going to say, and I apologize for taking matters into my own hands. I have discovered through my business dealings that when one is faced with a reluctant client one sometimes has to force the issue. Usually with rewarding results, as in this instance."

"No, Helmut. We need to—"

"Just a moment, dear. What was that, Reeves?"

Reeves was with Helmut and listening to their conversation! Anger made her hand tremble. The man was impossible. "Jordan, Reeves says 'good morning', and hopes that your feet aren't still hurting you." Helmut chuckled into the receiver.

Reeves had known that her feet were hurting her last night as he practically ran her home. "My feet are fine," she grated. "I really have to go now, Helmut." She

wasn't about to discuss personal matters over the telephone with Helmut while she knew Reeves was listening
avidly to every word with that knowing, derisive expression on his face.

"One more thing, darling, before you hang up. Reeves
is going to follow me around most of the day, taking
pictures in the office and at the board meeting this
afternoon. Tonight he wants to take pictures of us in a
relaxed, typically Swiss setting. I thought we'd take him
to Stadtkeller. It's for tourists, I know, but it's certainly
Swiss!"

"That sounds marvelous and I'm sure Mr. Grant will
enjoy it, but I must decline. I—"

"Nonsense. He specifically asked that you go with us.
He wants you in most of the pictures since you will soon
be my wife."

Damn! Reeves was instigating a farcical situation. He
must adore Neil Simon plays. She and Helmut were now
the unwilling players in such a comedy. "Helmut, please.
I—"

"Is there something wrong, Jordan?" Helmut's cheer-
ful voice changed to one of concern. "You sound distressed this morning. Aren't you well? Perhaps I should
come over and—"

"No!" she said sharply. The last thing she wanted was
for Reeves to know that he had upset her. And she didn't
want Helmut to see the violet shadows under her eyes
that testified to a sleepless night. He might jump to all the
wrong conclusions. He would demand an explanation for
her obvious depression. He would never understand that
she only wished to be left alone. But he *would* understand a simpering female, which she knew he thought her
to be.

"No, nothing's really wrong," she said, softening her voice to a childish whimper. "It's just that I was deliberating on what to wear tonight. I've never had my picture taken by a photographer with a reputation as renowned as Mr. Grant's." She virtually choked on the ridiculous words, but Helmut laughed into the phone.

"She's worried over what to wear," she heard him say to Reeves. Her slender fingers around the old-fashioned telephone tightened in agitation. "Darling, you'll look beautiful in anything, but keep it casual tonight. We'll be by to pick you up around eight. Things won't really be jumping at Stadtkeller until then. Good-bye for now." He hung up before she could reply. As was Helmut's habit, when he was finished speaking he considered the conversation to be concluded.

She replaced the telephone under the counter and tallied up the purchases of the middle-aged couple from Sioux Falls, South Dakota. The lady was buying two Agatha Christie mysteries and a copy of *The Sensuous Woman*. He had a James Bond book, a *Mad* magazine, and yesterday's *Chicago Tribune*. Would wonders never cease?

Desultorily, Jordan went through the day. Business was steady if not heavy. This was the end of September and the summer tourist season was waning. It wouldn't pick up again until those who came for winter sports passed through Lucerne. She sold newspapers, maps, paperbacks, magazines, and journals. She listened to tales of woe about the shortage of ice in virtually all of Europe, the taste and gastric dangers of the drinking water, the narrow roads (where were the interstate highways?), and the crazy way these "foreigners" drove an automobile. Sometimes Jordan hated to acknowledge her fellow countrymen. Too often they were brash, rude, critical, and ignorant to the point of hilarity.

At six o'clock she locked the door, put her CLOSED sign in the window, and pulled down the shade on the glass door. Wearily she trudged upstairs. She had two hours to prepare herself for the ordeal of the evening ahead but wasn't sure she would ever be ready for it.

She soaked in the deep, narrow tub. Unconsciously, she wondered how Reeves managed to fit his broad shoulders in most of the bath tubs in Europe and then decided that he probably took showers.

Impatiently she jerked her mind away from him and ticked off her wardrobe in her mind. What should she wear? She finally decided on a soft teal wool skirt and sweater. The skirt was full and fashionably hemmed and went well with her black suede boots. The outfit would be nothing spectacular without the triangular plaid woolen shawl that went with it. Six-inch fringe hung luxuriantly around the bottom. She put it over one shoulder and belted it at her waist with a wide gold belt. The corners of it almost reached the edge of her skirt. The prim "shopkeeper," as Reeves had called her, looked more like a high-fashion model. Indeed, she had bought the Laurent copy last year in a Paris boutique.

She shook her hair free of its confining bun and fluffed it around her face, letting it settle softly on her shoulders. She was misting Norell around her head when she heard the knock on the door. Hastily she grabbed her gray suede coat and the purse that matched her boots and went downstairs.

The door rattled slightly as she pulled it open. "Hello, darling. I was just telling Reeves that I wish I could persuade you to come live with me in the château and give up this dismal little shop and apartment." Helmut kissed her on the cheek and took both her hands in his, making note that she wore his ring. "Alas, Reeves, she's a morally stubborn woman. She refuses to engage in such goings on until after we are married."

Despite her determination to remain aloof, Jordan flushed hotly. It was true that Helmut had argued with her over her scruples against living with him until they were married. She had claimed that her need for independence was the reason. The fact was that she was in no hurry to sleep with Helmut. She had enjoyed his tender, passionate embraces, but they hadn't made her heart sing. Not like . . .

She swiftly looked at Reeves and saw his eyebrows cocked in incredulity. Think what you want, she longed to fling at him. It's true. I haven't slept with Helmut.

She had always imagined that Helmut would make love with the same economy of words and deeds with which he transacted a business deal. He would get straight to the point, waste no unnecessary time. It wouldn't be lingering and leisurely. He wouldn't stroke, and caress, and kiss, and tease just as much afterward as before. He wouldn't . . .

She pulled herself upright and said calmly, "Hello, Helmut." Rising on tiptoes, she kissed him softly on the mouth. Then, with a triumphant look, she turned to Reeves. "Good evening, Mr. Grant."

He stepped forward and took her hand. Helmut couldn't know, unless he read the shocked expression on Jordan's face, that Reeves's thumb was stroking her palm. "Under the circumstances, I think you should call me by my first name, don't you, Jordan?"

4

His words stunned her speechless and she could only stare, marveling at his daring. Then she realized that only he and she were cognizant of the "circumstances" to which he was referring.

To confirm her deduction, Helmut said heartily, "He's right, Jordan. Reeves will be with us constantly, for the next several days. Indeed, he may want to photograph you alone. By all means, let's be on a first-name basis."

She couldn't meet Reeves's mocking grin.

Helmut draped her coat around her shoulders, for even this early in the season the nights could be quite cold. They strolled through the alleyways until they reached a thoroughfare where Helmut's chauffeur was waiting with the silver Mercedes limousine.

Jordan found herself ensconced between the two men on the black velour seat. Though Helmut held her hand as it rested on his thigh, it was the other man she was painfully aware of.

Reeves was wearing jeans again, but this pair was creased and starched. A caramel-colored Cardin sport coat over a beige shirt molded to the breadth of his chest and shoulders. He had on highly polished cowboy boots. Perversely, he didn't look out of place, for jeans and Western boots were almost a uniform all over Europe these days for men and women alike.

When he leaned across her to speak to Helmut, she caught the brisk, clean-smelling fragrance of his shaving soap and cologne. It was pungent and potent, but not cloying, perfect for the man who was wearing it.

While the two men discussed some facet of Helmut's enterprises that Reeves found interesting, Jordan remained quiet and listened only to the inflection of Reeves's voice. He spoke with conviction and intelligence. Somehow her right shoulder had become sheltered beneath his left one, where it felt warmly secure. When he brought his arm back after making a gesture with his left hand, it skated across her breast.

Holding her breath, she slid her eyes toward him and met a gaze as alarmed and electrified as her own. Gratefully she felt the car slow down as they reached their destination.

Stadtkeller was a popular restaurant-nightclub in the city of Lucerne. An evening there was included in virtually every organized tour. The rustic tavern was loud, raucous, friendly. The specialty of the house was fondue, and while patrons gorged on the hard bread dipped in chafing dishes of melted cheese, they were entertained by performers in native costume.

The men wore lederhosen of gray suede trimmed with dark green leather with white, full-sleeved shirts. Knee-high socks with red tassels covered their legs, made muscular by mountain climbing. The women wore blouses embroidered in bright colors, black velvet basques laced tightly over their bosoms, and full skirts.

They sang, yodeled, danced folk dances, played the massive and unique alpenhorns—all to the enthusiastic endorsement of the crowd. Reeves snapped the shutter of his camera with a speed that awed Jordan. He changed lenses, filters, and film with machinelike accuracy. His film captured a toddling little girl with rosy cheeks and blond curly hair. She alternately stuffed bread or chocolate into her cherub mouth while clapping her hands excitedly in rhythm with the wheezing oomp-pa music.

"Who knows," Reeves said when he returned to the table and Helmut teased about his interest in the child, "I may sell an Alpine piece to *National Geographic*. Or she's pretty enough to go on a poster. I'll see how the pictures turn out. Anyway, I love kids. They're great photographic subjects in any culture."

He rubbed his hands together eagerly after he closed up his camera for the night and dug into the stringy, chewy cheese and hard bread with a healthy appetite.

Helmut poured white wine into their chafing dish and mixed it with the cheese. Soon all three of them were feeling mellow and laughing at the adventurous stories Reeves regaled them with.

"Would you like coffee before we take Jordan home?" Helmut asked when they left the noisy nightclub.

"Sounds great."

Helmut signaled his chauffeur to follow them with the car and they walked a few blocks to a restaurant across the street from the lake shore. They sacrificed sitting outside because of the cold and went inside to the quiet, elegant ambiance of the restaurant, where Helmut and Jordan were formally greeted by the maître d'.

"I know Jordan wants hot chocolate. Reeves?" Helmut asked.

"Coffee," he said.

When their waiter brought back their order, Jordan sipped at the steamy mug topped with foamy whipped cream. Never had she enjoyed dairy products so much until she came to Switzerland. They were unsurpassed anyplace in the world.

She ran the tip of her tongue along her foam-flecked lips, but when she sat back Reeves saw a drop of the whipped cream in the corner of her mouth. Without even thinking on it, he reached toward it and flicked it away, then licked the cream off his finger. They smiled, caught up in a private, intimate moment that hadn't been planned, but had happened on its own and for no other reason than that they had looked at each other.

Helmut, who had been lighting a cigarette, didn't see the reason for the silence he interrupted by saying, "Jordan has one vice, I've found. She has a penchant for our Swiss chocolate. I fear that in her old age she'll grow quite fat."

"I will not!" Jordan exclaimed heatedly, and they laughed at her vehemence. Embarrassed, she went back to her cup of chocolate and drained it while they lingered over their coffee.

"Why don't you take Reeves across the bridge," Helmut suggested.

"What?" she asked too quickly, startled.

"By now you know the history of it as well as I," Helmut said. "I'll sit here and drink another cup of coffee and smoke another cigarette while you take Reeves across the bridge and back. You haven't yet seen it, have you, Reeves?"

Reeves wasn't looking at Helmut. He was staring at Jordan. Finally he answered, "No, I haven't seen it except at a distance. I'd love to know everything about it."

Jordan shot him a quelling look. "We can wait until you're finished, then we'll all go," she said to Helmut.

"Darling, you know that I despise sight-seeing in general. Be hospitable to our guest for me."

"Very well," she said, standing up abruptly. Better to get it over with. "Let's go," she said as ungraciously as she could without raising Helmut's suspicions.

She reached for her coat, but Reeves was too quick and grabbed it out of the vacant chair. He held it for her as she slipped into the sleeves. "We'll be back shortly, Helmut," she said, placing a hand on his shoulder.

"Take your time." He reached up and patted her hand. "I may have two cigarettes."

As Reeves held the door of the restaurant open for her, she hurried past him, cramming her hands deep into her coat pockets and hunching her shoulders against the chill. She stepped out into the street, daringly crossed it in front of a honking tourist bus, and reached the other side almost at a run.

Reeves pulled up beside her and clasped her elbow. "Is this to be the whirlwind tour?"

"Don't you dare try to be cute with me after the things you said last night."

"You're not being hospitable," he chided in a singsong voice.

She ground her teeth. "You wanted to see the bridge, so okay, I'll show you the damn bridge," she said unreasonably. "Why didn't you just decline Helmut's offer and sit there and smoke a cigarette with him?"

"I've quit smoking again." He grinned. "Besides, I really want to see the bridge."

By now they had reached one of the two covered bridges that spanned the Reuss River. The river divided the city into the modern town on the west and the old town on the east. The clear water gurgled and rushed under their feet as they stepped onto the ancient wooden bridge.

In a bored, flat, tourist-guide voice, Jordan said, "The bridge dates back to the Middle Ages. As you will see overhead there are myriad panels. Each panel has two paintings, one on each side, that depict an event of regional history. The paintings date back to the early sixteen hundreds."

"Very interesting," he said dryly.

"The Lake of Lucerne covers over forty square miles. Four Swiss cantons, or states, border it. It—"

"Jordan," he said harshly, and jerked her around to face him. "Why aren't you living with Helmut?"

"None of your business," she shouted. When her

voice reverberated loudly from the ceiling of the covered bridge, she lowered it. "None of your business."

"Yes it is."

"No it isn't."

"Yes it is, dammit."

His hands were digging into the flesh of her upper arms and, in spite of her heavy clothing, his grip was painful. When she flinched, he realized how hard he was holding her and let her go immediately. She continued walking as if he hadn't spoken.

"Why?" he persisted.

She spun around to face him, glad that there was no one else on the bridge at the moment. "Because I don't want to. I don't believe in living with someone without being married to him." That expressive eyebrow rose in disbelief. Frustrated, she said, "The other night was an . . . an accident. I didn't plan it, nor did you. It just . . . happened." She didn't look at him, but she didn't move away either. He seemed to hold her like a magnet. She could feel his eyes boring into the top of her head as she stared at the toes of his boots. "I told you then that I don't . . . don't sleep around. If you didn't believe me then, you won't now either. I don't care if you do or not." But she did.

"Do you love him?"

"Helmut?"

"Are there others?"

She sighed in exasperation. "No. There are no others." He completely disoriented her. She couldn't think clearly, especially with him standing so close. Trembling fingers rubbed her forehead, which had begun to pound with the tension from within.

"I don't love Helmut. At least, not in that way. He's

fun, he's charming, polite, and, yes, rich. I can't deny that I was flattered when he began seeing me. I was. Any woman would be. But don't you see, Reeves?" Now she looked up at him imploringly. "I'm a novelty. He has everything in the world he could possibly want. He plays. He goes on lavish vacations. He buys impulsively and compulsively. Right now I'm like a new toy. I'm not rich, not a jet-setter, not a socialite. When he tires of me, that will be it."

"If that's true, why did you consent to marry him?"

"I haven't ever exactly *consented*—I just haven't adamantly *refused*. Since I realize I'm a temporary fascination, I haven't pressed the point. My constant arguing to the contrary would only increase his determination to have me. Understand? Helmut, despite his Old World charm, is overbearing when he wants something. He only hears what he wants to. He hasn't given me a chance to tell him how I feel."

"And how do you feel? I mean, if the novelty should wear off tomorrow, how would you feel if he did as you predict and dropped you?"

"I told you, I've never intended to marry him. I never intend to marry anyone."

"Why? Because of Charles?"

"Yes, partially."

"Partially? Do you have something against the institution of marriage?"

His pious tone stung. "No. Do you?" she snapped. "You're not married either." Then a thunderbolt struck her. She looked up at him with remorseful eyes. "Are you?" she asked timorously.

"No. I was once. A long time ago."

"What happened?"

"Would I get clouted if I said, 'None of your business'?"

She laughed. "Probably."

He chuckled, then said seriously, "She didn't understand why I wanted to go to Vietnam 'to take pictures,' as she put it. She filed for divorce soon after I left. We had been married less than a year."

"Oh." Jordan turned away from him and walked to the railing of the bridge, listening to the water that churned under it.

"Jordan." When he spoke he was standing close behind her. He was as close as he could get without touching her. "Jordan," he repeated.

"Yes?"

"Look at me."

No! She knew that if she did she would want to be held tight against him. Just as she had feared touching his hand that first night for no reason other than a friendly handshake, she feared looking at him now. It had been wrong for them then and it still was. He had his work, his ambition, which literally went worldwide. She had her tiny space on the planet and guarded it jealously, afraid of letting anyone disturb the equanimity she had so carefully constructed.

His hands were on her shoulders and he was turning her toward him. With a now familiar gesture, he lifted her chin with his finger. "I like what you're wearing."

That was the last thing she had expected him to say. "Thank you," was all she could think of to respond.

"You look great in clothes," he said. "This, however, is a trifle bulky. I can't see your figure." His hands unbuttoned her coat and slipped inside. "I liked you much better in the slacks and sweater you were wearing the other night. They showed everything to full advantage."

He ducked his head and nuzzled his face in the hollow of her neck, which had, without instruction, arched up to meet him.

"Reeves," she breathed, "don't."

Her protest was so feeble that he didn't even honor it. "I remember what you look like in that pale pink sweater and I remember what you look like without it." His voice was becoming unsteady as his lips skimmed her face, brushed across her mouth. His hands were under the shawl now, seeking the curves of her breasts. When he found them his moan of gratification matched hers.

Into her hair he murmured, "I like the way you dress, the way you move. I like to watch you eat and drink. Especially hot chocolate. I like the sound of your voice. I love the way you feel. I love the way you touch me. I love the way you smell, the way your skin tastes—"

"Reeves, we shouldn't. This isn't right," she said against his insistent mouth.

"Let me hold you. Let me kiss you. And then tell me it isn't right. Jordan," he rasped as his hands closed over the soft mounds beneath her sweater, "I dare you to tell me this isn't right."

When his mouth melded with hers, it was impossible to think of a reasonable protest, much less to utter one. His lips burned through hers, and she was doomed to die under their fire. He countenanced no resistance, no reluctance. He sipped at her lips until they became malleable to his will and then he parted them with a gentle thrust of his tongue.

He savored her mouth, one moment ravaging it, the next soothing it with lips and tongue. One arm curved around her back and drew her inexorably against him, while the other hand continued to smooth over her sweater-clad chest.

"Why did you wear that damn bra?" he growled against her ear, and worried the lobe with his teeth.

"I—"

"It doesn't matter," he whispered. "I can still feel you through it." And his inquisitive fingers proved his point.

"Reeves?" She was barely capable of speaking, so fine was the passionate web he had spun around her.

"Yes?"

"Reeves?" she breathed.

The echo of thudding footsteps came to them out of the darkness. An instant later they were aware of Helmut's voice calling out, "Jordan, Reeves?"

They looked at each other and froze. Reeves was calm, cool, unaffected. He waited for her reaction. Jordan was alarmed. She didn't feel any grand love for Helmut, but she didn't want to hurt or humiliate him either. His personality couldn't take such a blow. She jumped away from Reeves, straightening her clothing, and took a few hastening steps toward the direction of the voice. "We're here, Helmut."

"You were gone so long, I thought you might have lost your way," he said humorously as he drew closer and soon stepped into a circle of light nearby.

"No, we . . . I was just telling Reeves one of the legends you told me about William Tell," she said, lying badly.

Helmut, secure and confident of himself, didn't notice

the prevarication. "You must be cold, my dear. You're shivering. Button up your coat. Perhaps we should see you home. Did you enjoy the tour, Reeves?"

There was an unendurable pause before he answered, and Jordan held her breath. She looked at him with pleading eyes and was startled to see the brittle emerald glare that pierced the darkness. "Yes," he replied to Helmut's question. "I found it most informative and entertaining. I can't vouch for the veracity of everything Jordan told me. Some of the tales are just too outlandish."

Her breath caught in her throat. He didn't believe her! *Why?*

Helmut chuckled. "I'll admit that some of the fables about our local heroes are a bit farfetched."

"Farfetched indeed," Reeves said.

He left them at the end of the bridge, saying he preferred to walk the rest of the way to his hotel.

"Do you think you'll have any problems?" Jordan asked the young man anxiously.

He smiled at her with cool confidence. "I think I can manage the shop in your absence, Mrs. Hadlock."

He was an employee of Helmut's who worked in one of the offices as an accountant. Last night, when Helmut had brought her home, he had informed her that she was to meet him and Reeves for breakfast the next day.

"We have quite an expedition planned. We're going up on Pilatus—"

"Helmut," she interrupted. "I have a business to run. You and Reeves will have to get along without me tomorrow."

She was angry and upset with what had just happened

on the bridge. Now she was being told she would have to suffer another day with the man who continued to ridicule and insult her. One moment she was pouring out her innermost feelings to him and he listened with seemingly sincere empathy. The next moment he was kissing her as though he'd die if he didn't. Then, when she was quivering with a desire he had kindled, he abruptly spurned her, all but calling her a liar—and worse.

She'd had enough. She didn't want to see him again, much less spend a day with him. "I won't be able to go tomorrow," she said firmly.

"Of course you will, darling," Helmut countered with customary high-handedness. "I'm sending someone over to take care of your little shop for you. You needn't worry about it. You'll be able to play all day."

His manipulation of her life was suddenly becoming intolerable. If he managed his fiancée like this, how would he treat a wife? His condescending remark about her "little shop" was insulting. She did a tremendous business. Her company held her shop up as the proto- type for all the others. She was proud of the services she provided to English-speaking tourists. Why should he belittle it?

"I don't want to be gone tomorrow, Helmut. I'm needed here," she said stubbornly. "You may think that, compared to your conglomerate, this bookstore is noth- ing, but it's very important to me."

"Jordan, Jordan," he said softly. "I've offended you and I'm sorry." His tone of voice carried all the conde- scension of one speaking to a recalcitrant child. "Don't be obtuse. Please, darling. If you don't come with us, Reeves will think you don't like him, or that you're camera shy. When you become my wife, Jordan, you'll be photographed constantly."

Right then she should have told him that she had no intention of becoming his wife and calmly returned his ring. Instead her mind had locked in on what he had said about Reeves thinking she might not like him. Or that she was camera shy. He wouldn't think that, but he might construe that she was a coward. If she didn't go with them on these photographic sessions, he might think she was hiding from him out of shame or cowardice. She wouldn't give him that satisfaction.

"All right, Helmut," she said absently as he kissed her neck in what he considered to be a stirring caress. "I'll meet you tomorrow. Where and when?"

They had set the time and place and now she was giving the prompt accountant last-minute instructions. Ruefully, she thought that when she returned she would probably find that the sales for that day were higher than ever before and that the shop was in better shape than when she had left it.

She wended her way through the alleys carrying her fur ski parka. It was a bright, clear morning, but she knew that at the top of Mount Pilatus it would be much colder and she had come prepared. Her black corduroy jeans hugged her hips and legs tightly. The red sweater with the high, rolled collar was soft and clung to the gentle swell of her breasts. She had tucked a cap into the pocket of her parka in case she needed it on the mountaintop.

Helmut and Reeves were waiting for her at the appointed restaurant and they ate a hearty American breakfast. Jordan drank one cup of coffee and then indulged in a pot of chocolate lavishly topped with whipped cream.

The men were dressed as casually as she, though Helmut's idea of "casual" was dress slacks, a sport coat, a cashmere sweater, and a sealskin overcoat. Reeves looked like he was about to ride the ranges of a cattle ranch, wearing everything a well-dressed cowboy needed except the hat. After he had finished eating and while they were waiting for Helmut's cigarette to burn down, he checked his equipment.

He had greeted Jordan cordially when she arrived, following Helmut's lead of kissing her on the cheek. This was Europe. Everyone kissed everyone else on the cheek. Helmut thought nothing of it. Indeed, he was glad that the American photojournalist obviously found his fiancée attractive.

But Jordan hadn't taken the salutation lightly. Her heart stumbled around in her throat and she had to hold herself rigid to keep from swaying against Reeves as he pulled away.

Reeves, too, had exhibited extreme control. He had longed to pull her into his arms and kiss her fully on that appealing mouth. That fleeting taste of her had only acted as an appetizer and he was starved for more.

The trio created a slight commotion when they boarded the cable car at the base of Mount Pilatus. Helmut's chauffeur ushered them through the crowd. Tourists and natives alike were intrigued by Reeves and his cameras and watched in fascination as the three situated themselves in one of the small cars. Reeves placed his equipment on one of the four chairs while Helmut and Jordan sat facing him.

"How long will we be in this car?" he asked, checking his light meter as he held it in front of their faces.

"About twenty minutes," Helmut told him. "Then we

get out at a station halfway up the mountain and take another, larger car, one that holds about forty people, the rest of the way to the summit. All in all, it takes about forty-five minutes."

Reeves looked a little green around the gills as their car lurched forward. They were being hauled away from the ground and up the side of the mountain that stood sentinel over the city and the Lake of Lucerne.

Reeves switched lenses several times; he twirled the focus rings; he changed the filters that snapped onto the end of his lens; and the shutter clicked incessantly. And all the while he was talking to them, putting them at ease, making them forget that camera. Even as Jordan relaxed and began to behave normally, she was aware of his talent.

"You're great subjects," he commented as he put his camera back in the case after exchanging a new roll of film with a used one. "I'll do some more when we get to the top."

"Look behind you, Reeves," Helmut said. "There's a spectacular view of the lake. To your right you'll see my château."

Jordan thought he hesitated a moment before he looked behind him at the picture-book panorama of the city and the lake far below.

"Yeah, that's beautiful," Reeves said shakily as he whipped his head back around.

Jordan suppressed a giggle. He was afraid of heights! He didn't look behind him again, but kept his eyes straight ahead, where the mountain loomed behind Helmut and her. Every once in a while they would hear a group of backpackers as they made their way up the mountain. Jordan would lean out the railing of the open-air car and wave to them, shouting greetings in several languages. Reeves remained as motionless as stone and gripped the edge of his chair.

They arrived at the midway point and had only a short wait for one of the larger cable cars. They filed aboard with the other sightseers and Helmut immediately headed for a position near the wide windows.

Reeves held back and clutched a pole in the center of the car. Jordan smiled as she stood with him. "You should have said you're afraid of heights," she teased.

"I'm not afraid. I'm petrified," he admitted with a self-derisive laugh.

"We don't have to go the rest of the way," she said.

He looked out the window of the cable car toward the top of the mountain and gulped. Fog shrouded the summit, so that the frighteningly narrow cable, looking like a thread, disappeared into the cloud.

"No. I'll be fine once we get on solid ground. It's being suspended that I can't stand."

"But surely you fly all the time. How do you handle that?"

"Usually with a good belt of Scotch. Then I started reading about so many people getting plastered on airplanes that if an accident does occur they're useless in trying to save themselves. Which is even more terrifying. So, I white-knuckle it." He grinned boyishly. "Unless I have a hand to hold."

He reached under the fur jacket she held in the crook of her arm and took her hand, squeezing it lightly. She returned the pressure and they smiled at each other. Reeves looked toward Helmut, who was chatting amia-

5

~~~~~~~~~~~~

He doesn't watch you very carefully. Doesn't he ever get jealous?"

She looked at Helmut, who was blessing the two women with one of his dazzling smiles. "No. He's too self-confident to think that I'd be interested in anyone else."

"He's a fool." He spoke with such intensity that she looked up into the green eyes that flashed with some emotion she couldn't name. "No man should ever take a beautiful woman for granted."

His eyes dropped to her mouth. The lips were slightly

parted. Her delicate pink tongue lay just beyond the row of small teeth and he could recall vividly how it felt against his own. He had kissed many women all over the world. But as soon as the kisses stopped, he forgot them.

Not with Jordan. He knew exactly how she would taste if he kissed her now. Once her initial caution had been overcome, he had been surprised at the unbridled way she responded to him. It wasn't feigned. It was as though Jordan's passion had lain dormant in her for a long while. Suddenly it had roiled to the surface, and he had been the lucky instigator of that freedom.

Or was that part of a game she played? His eyes swept back up to hers, but he read no deceit there. He was certain that if he pulled her into his arms now she wouldn't resist. But what would it mean to her? Was she playing games? Did she know the power she had over his mind and body?

He hadn't realized he had voiced the words until he heard himself say, "And you are a beautiful woman, Jordan."

A tiny tremor shook her mouth. "Do you think so?"

"Yes. And you're courageous. This is the second time you've saved my life. Once during a thunderstorm and now on this treacherous mountain." His tone was bantering now and she answered in kind.

"This heated, comfortable, highly technical cable car is hardly treacherous," she countered.

"But the thunderstorm was fearsome."

"Yes," she conceded. "But you know what they say. 'Any port in a storm.'"

He laughed. "Hardly. I doubt that if you'd been a gray-haired grandmother I'd have . . . thanked . . . you in quite the same way."

"Then you were only expressing gratitude?"

He was still smiling, but the expression changed character. It became intimate, tender, heart-melting. "No. Gratitude had little or nothing to do with it."

They bumped together slightly when the cable car jolted to a halt. A low groan was emitted from Reeves's throat as her fingers, still entwined with his beneath the cover of her parka, inadvertently pressed against his body. Jordan gasped softly and looked at him guiltily when she realized what she was touching. The crowd, eager to disembark, formed a tight, wiggling circle around them, and for long, agonizing moments they couldn't move.

"I'm sorry," she whispered, sneaking a shy look up into his face. Her cheeks were flaming scarlet.

"Don't apologize on my account." The corner of his mouth lifted in a provocative grin that made her heart thud painfully in her chest.

When the crowd began to thin, Reeves let go of her hand and they made their way to the sliding door of the cable car. Helmut was kissing the hands of the two girls in turn and saying in French, "I hope you have a most enjoyable holiday." The girls twittered and fluttered their eyelashes as they waved good-bye to him. "There you are," he said when he saw Jordan and Reeves step out the door. "I had a most pleasant trip up. Quite nice girls. Did you two manage to amuse yourselves?"

Jordan nearly choked, but Reeves answered easily, "It was thrilling."

Jordan knew well what "it" he was referring to. His eyes twinkled at her mischievously and she wasn't successful in hiding her secret smile.

The summit of Mount Pilatus was blanketed in clouds.

In fact, if one stood still he could feel a fine, icy mist settling on his face. The weather, however, didn't dampen the carnival atmosphere. Music blared from speakers mounted on light poles. Tourists milled about, browsing in the gift shop, ordering sandwiches and drinks from the snack bar, and competing for the open-air tables scattered around the area. A melodic voice periodically announced in several languages the departure of the cable cars.

Reeves was busy with his camera, taking pictures of Helmut against the backdrop of snow-covered peaks on the near and far horizons.

When business was taken care of, the three sat around a table in the indoor lounge and Helmut ordered cappuccino for them.

"Well, now I can boast having been on top of one of the Alps," Reeves said.

"Not quite the top," Helmut said.

"What?"

Jordan explained. "To get to the actual summit you have to climb some stairs up about sixty more feet. There is a platform up there."

Reeves seemed disinterested and she prodded, "Come on. Let's do it."

"Climb up there?" he asked, instantly alarmed.

"Yes!"

He glowered at her from under his eyebrows. "I don't think so," he mumbled.

"You really should, Reeves," Helmut chimed in. "It's quite spectacular."

Reeves still hedged and took another sip of his drink. "I don't—"

"You're not afraid, are you?" Jordan taunted.

"No," he growled.

"Well, then, let's go." She stood up and shrugged back into her parka, which she had put on as soon as she stepped off the cable car. She whipped her knitted cap out of the pocket and pulled it over her hair, low on her forehead.

Reeves really didn't have a choice. "All right," he grumbled as he stood up and pulled on his fleece-lined shearling coat.

"Coming, Helmut?" Jordan asked when he made no move to get out of his chair.

"No, you *children* run along. The doctor cautions me that a man of my age should take it a little slower."

Reeves and Jordan laughed. He looked anything but decrepit as he sat there sipping his cappuccino, his legs crossed, one Gucci loafer swinging negligently.

Reeves hung his camera around his neck as Jordan virtually dragged him out of the coffee shop. "I could easily throttle you. I don't want to do this," he said as they crossed the compound toward the stairs that would take them to the top.

"You said you weren't afraid as long as you were on solid ground."

"I lied."

"There's nothing to worry about. The platform only sways a few degrees and the nearest plateau is only a thousand feet down."

He paled significantly, but she only laughed and pulled him along behind her. They had climbed about half the stairs when they stopped momentarily to catch their breath in the thin air. He looked at her seriously, took her by the shoulders, and said solemnly, "Jordan, I want you to remember one thing if something should happen to me."

"Reeves—"

"Promise me," he said urgently.

"All right," she vowed. "I promise."

"If I should go toppling off the side of this mountain, try to get the camera from around my neck and catch the shot."

She swung at him with her fist, but he dodged it, laughing and holding off her pummeling fists with one hand while he drew her against him with the other arm.

"You devil!" she cried. "I thought you were serious."

"I was! You'd probably win the Pulitzer."

She spun around huffily, but they were both laughing as they trudged up the remainder of the way.

When they reached the top, Reeves took one sweeping look, said, "Very nice," and then turned back toward the stairs.

Jordan reached out and grabbed his elbow. "No you don't. I didn't climb all the way up here for nothing." It was noticeably colder so she zipped her parka together and stuffed her hands into the fur-lined pockets. She leaned back against the rail and breathed in the cold air.

"Stay right there," Reeves commanded as he brought his camera up to his eyes. He moved closer, stepped away, held the Nikon first horizontally, then vertically. The shutter snapped with a hypnotic cadence. Jordan loved to watch the way he moved, crouching, standing straight, leaning back with his hips thrust forward, leaning forward. It was a masculine ballet.

"You make a very pretty picture, Jordan. I love you in that red. It looks great against the white and black fur.

The sweater and cap against the gray-white background. Super . . ." His voice trailed off as he took another series of pictures. "The cold has made your cheeks rosy and I like the black wisps of hair blowing out from under the cap. Great. Exhale now so I can see the vapor. Great. Turn your head to the left a little. There. Lower your chin. Smile. Now serious. Perfect. Nice."

When he ran out of film, he capped his lens and cautiously walked over toward the rail. "Helmut might not like seeing so many pictures of me in an article about him," she said.

Reeves moved closer and paused before he said, "Helmut will never see these pictures. They're for me alone."

Then he kissed her. They didn't even pretend that they didn't want to. She came into his arms willingly and tilted her head back to greet his descending mouth.

Their breath almost crystallized in the cold air as they came together. His mouth was hot when it opened over hers and still tasted of the brandy that had laced their cappuccino.

Her hands slipped inside his coat, which had remained open, and traveled up the length of his back, idly exploring the hard muscles that rippled under the soft flannel shirt.

"I'm going to give you just ten or fifteen minutes to stop doing that," he said against her lips, not removing the pressure of his.

"No, I'm going to stop now," she said as she pulled away from him. Their kisses were becoming embarrassingly impassioned and there were other tourists on the lookout platform.

"Damn!" he cursed under his breath.

She laughed. "What was the worst situation you've ever been in when you were working?" She resorted to casual conversation, for his hands were sensuously stroking the fur collar that reached up under her chin.

"Whew, that's a tough question. Vietnam was hell. Felt like it. Smelled like it. Cambodia was hideous. I guess the worst situation, though, was El Salvador. I've never been so scared in my life. Everybody was shooting everybody else and asking whose side they were on later."

"Reeves, why do you do it? Journalists get killed too, just like soldiers." She quivered when she thought of him bloody and wounded.

He shrugged. "I don't know. It's a compulsion that's hard to explain. I have to be in the big, thick middle of it, or I might miss that best shot, *the* picture of the decade, like the soldiers raising the flag on Iwo Jima."

She didn't really understand his drive, but she shook her head ponderingly. "I know you've won prestigious awards for your work, but what's your favorite picture—the one *you* like the best?"

"I haven't taken it yet," he said.

She should have known by the way he had her pinned against the rail with his own body and the low, tense pitch of his voice that his mind was no longer on the subject they were discussing.

"My favorite picture is going to be one of you. Naked."

"Reeves!" she grated, and looked around hastily, hoping that none of the other tourists spoke English.

"Let's see, how should I do it?" he asked with a feigned objectivity. One eyelid was lowered as he considered her clinically. "In a field of flowers? No, that's too sweet, too innocent."

"Thanks a lot! I—"

"Maybe lying on your back on a black satin sheet with your arms flung over your head," he mused aloud.

"Reeves, will you please—"

"No, that's too . . . too blatant. Not like you. Not your style. Let's see." He squinted harder as he stared at her and she felt herself flush all over. The topic was far too bold, and she shouldn't be standing here letting him talk about her that way. Still, the prospect of posing for him was wickedly attractive and exciting.

"I know," he said slowly. "You'll be on a wide bed. I'll shoot it through gauze so you'll look kind of ethereal. You'll be lying on your side facing the camera. Should you be draped or totally naked?" he mused aloud. "Totally naked, I think. One arm will be stretched out in front of you and the other is folded over your chest. Only one breast—"

"Reeves," she groaned, and buried her face against his shirt front.

"Your hair will be tousled, as if you'd just awakened when someone came in the room. It's your lover. And your eyes are wide and silently asking him if he's going to make love to you. But you know the answer." His voice had roughened and his face had lowered until it was inches from her own. "The answer is 'Yes!' Yes."

His parted lips met hers hungrily as he drew her to him. His tongue penetrated the barrier of her lips and teeth and pillaged the inside of her mouth. Each honeyed crevice was robbed. An unsatisfied moan rumbled deep in his chest as he pulled her tighter against him. She gasped, and even his befuddled senses could tell it wasn't a desire-inspired reaction. He pulled back quickly. "What is it?" he asked.

"Your camera," she cried piteously.

He looked down to see that his camera hung directly in front of her breasts. "I'm sorry," he said. "I didn't realize."

"Neither did I for a while." She stood up on tiptoes to kiss him quickly on the lips. "Reeves, we must go."

He looked off in the distance at the spectacular view of the Alpine mountain range. "I know," he said regretfully. "I—" He broke off suddenly and cocked his head to listen. "What in the hell is that?"

Jordan had heard the sound too, and smiled. To his distress, she began to walk along the railing, leaning over it now and then. He didn't know what she was looking at, for the clouds separated them from the ground far below. "What—"

"There!" she exclaimed. "Come here quickly before the clouds hide them again." She pointed down the side of the mountain and, through the hazy clouds, he saw a green mountain pasture several hundred feet below them. There was a sizable herd of cattle grazing in the pasture.

"Cattle?" he asked, puzzled.

"Milk cows. You were hearing their cow bells," she explained.

"I thought those heavy things on the thick leather straps were only for the tourists to buy as souvenirs," he said as he continued to gaze down at the strange but picturesque sight.

"They are. But they're also very useful. A cow can hardly get lost in the mountains if she's wearing one of those bells. And the herd usually follows the lead of the one wearing the large bell."

"Well, whadaya know?" Reeves said. He looked at her closely and murmured softly, "For a moment there, I thought I was so close to heaven that I was hearing the angels sing."

"Well, you are pretty close to heaven. Mount Pilatus is—"

"I wasn't referring to the height of the mountain," he said.

Color bathed her cheeks as she looked away and started for the stairs. "I knew what you meant," was all she said as he took her hand.

For variety's sake they took the cog railroad down the other side of the mountain. It was Helmut's decision, but Reeves gratefully accepted it.

Henri, the chauffeur, was waiting with the limousine at the cog railroad station. "Oh, I was hoping we could go back on one of the ferries," Jordan said with disappointment. The ferries did a thriving business on the Lake of Lucerne. They were used by commuters and tourists alike. "I know it takes a long time with all of the stops, but it is always such fun."

"Then by all means take Reeves with you if you want to ride on one of the ferries," Helmut said generously. "For myself, I prefer the luxury of the automobile and Henri's driving. I've had enough tourism for the day." He turned to Reeves. "What do you think? Would you enjoy taking one of the boats? It will be at least an hour until you return to Lucerne."

"Fine," Reeves said. "What time are you meeting with that Italian manufacturer?"

"Four o'clock."

"I'd like to sit in on that if you don't mind, just for some background information."

"I don't mind at all. Why don't you and Jordan take

the ferry, see her home, and then come to the offices. You'll have plenty of time."

"Won't you please come, too, Helmut?" Jordan asked. She didn't want to appear to be too happy over being alone with Reeves.

"No, my dear. As much as I've enjoyed having Reeves with us, I have neglected some things on my desk. This will give me an opportunity to see to them. *Au revoir,*" he said, and kissed her tenderly on the lips.

His lips were cool and firm, so different from Reeves's warm, moist, yielding lips. Helmut's kiss didn't transport her into another sphere where she slowly, but inevitably, lost touch with the one she lived in. It didn't cause tiny ripples, like the aftershocks of an earthquake, to make her insides tremble.

He pulled away from her. "I'll call you later, darling."

"All right. Thank you for a lovely morning," she said, and was ashamed for being so insincere. Helmut had had nothing to do with the loveliness of the day.

He waved them good-bye as Henri held open the door to the sleek Mercedes. They were alone. Reeves stood in the queue to buy their tickets. They were jostled by the crowd, who waited while the ferry docked and disembarked its passengers. And they were unaware of everything except each other. Only the stampeding throng that scrambled aboard the ferry brought them out of their shared trance.

They were scurrying and laughing amidst the crowd when they found a small table on the upper open-air deck and claimed it as their own. They piled their coats in one of the extra chairs and Reeves's camera equipment in the other to discourage anyone from joining them.

Reeves bought them sandwiches and candy out of

vending machines and they sipped coffee that was served at the snack bar on the lower deck.

They sat together at the small table, unconscious of the milling tourists, the frequent stops for passenger exchanges, the chattering of several languages, aware only of each other. The day was gorgeous. The lake was azure placidity. But had the climate not been optimum, neither would have noticed, for they basked in the sunny glow of each other.

"Tell me all there is to know about Jordan Hadlock. What was your maiden name, by the way?" Reeves asked as he leaned forward and took her hand where it lay on the Formica table top.

"Simms. Why?" she asked, laughing.

He shrugged and smiled that boyish grin that by now she knew well. "I don't know. Just curious. I want to know everything about you."

Self-consciously, she looked down at their clasped hands. She thought of the exciting life he led and the other women he must meet every day and her life seemed to pale to insignificance. "There isn't much to tell. I think you know all there is to know."

"Tell me about your family."

She smiled. "My parents are lovely. Dad is a regional representative for a publishing house. Mother has always been a homemaker."

"Siblings?"

"One who died at birth a few years after I was born. No others."

"You told me that you were married for four years." She nodded. "Why didn't you have any children?"

"Charles didn't want any."

"But you did."

Was he clairvoyant? She ducked her head in self-consciousness. "Yes, I wanted children. Now I see that it wasn't meant to be."

Her wanting a family had been a source of contention between Charles and her. He hadn't wanted children to "slow him down." "When my ship comes in and we're on easy street, there'll be plenty of time for kids." But that time had never come and neither had the family that Jordan so longed for. In retrospect, she supposed that it was just as well. She wouldn't have wanted a child to grow up in the impermanence that existed in her marriage. She raised her eyes amd met Reeves's intent stare.

He was acutely aware of the sadness that had settled in her eyes, so he directed the conversation elsewhere. "Did your parents mind your coming over here?"

She pondered the question as her thumb stroked the light brown hairs that sprinkled the back of his hand. "Yes, they did, I'm sure. But they made no arguments to stop me. I think they understood why I had to leave. For a while anyway. Too, there had never been an excess of money in our house. I wasn't deprived, by any means, but I think they always felt guilty because they couldn't afford to send me to Europe when some of my schoolmates went after graduation. I even worked to help put myself through college. They wanted me to have this opportunity."

She glanced out over the lake with its sparkling blue water. The foothills rose around it, still green and dotted with quaint chalets. As charming as it was, she felt a wave of homesickness for her parents and her homeland. One couldn't stay away too long without missing it terribly. She roused herself and brought her eyes back to Reeves, who was watching her closely. "What about you? Do you have a family?"

"Dad is deceased. Mother is remarried to a wonderful gentleman, a retired grocer, who treats her like a queen. I have one kid sister who is in law school. God help the judicial system when she is let loose in it," he chuckled.

And so the hour flew by while they revealed aspects of their lives, past and present. Anyone watching might have thought they were lovers, for they never looked at anyone else. Indeed, they seemed unaware of anyone else.

During a break in their conversation, Reeves said, "Jordan, I just want to know one thing."

His tone was so serious that she felt a prickle of alarm. "Yes?" she asked hesitantly.

"Do you know when we're supposed to get off this boat?"

She burst into laughter. He joined her and they laughed just for the sheer joy of doing it together. Her gray eyes were swimming with tears of mirth when she answered, "The next stop is ours. We'd better start gathering up our things."

They walked down the gangplank arm in arm, still talking privately. Jordan happened to glance up and saw Henri, Helmut's chauffeur, scanning the crowd. She stepped away from the arm across her shoulders just as Henri spotted them.

"Mrs. Hadlock, I have a message for you from Mr. Eckherdt," the uniformed man said in halting English when he stood before them. "Mr. Eckherdt asked me to see you home. He has been invited to dinner this evening by a business associate and he wishes you to accompany him. He said to dress semiformally. He'll pick you up at seven thirty."

As he spoke, he had been escorting them through the crowd toward the parked car. Now he held the back door open for her and Reeves. Not knowing what to do, she turned toward Reeves with a bewildered, helpless expression on her face. They had planned that he would come to her apartment after his meeting with Helmut since she had no plans for the evening. What was she to do?

"Reeves . . . ?"

She wanted him to say that it was all right, that he understood. Instead she watched as his eyes, which had been lit up with laughter, turn icy. His mouth thinned into a grim line as he stood there and stared at her.

Nervously she licked her lips and said, "I . . . I have to go. He . . . Maybe sometime tonight I'll be able to talk to him. I . . ."

"Never mind, Jordan. It doesn't matter," he said in a cold, hard voice. "I understand perfectly." His tone indicated that he didn't understand at all. He was furious. The tight set of his facial muscles testified to that.

Henri stepped forward and bowed slightly. "Mr. Grant, I'm to take you to Mr. Eckherdt's offices as soon as I've dropped Mrs. Hadlock at her apartment."

"No thank you, Henri," Reeves said, declining the offer. He wasn't looking at the chauffeur, however. He was still glaring at Jordan. "I always make my own decisions."

Without another word, but with a scathing look at Jordan, he stalked away through the stragglers, who were trying to get to the ferry before it was launched again.

6

The evening dragged on interminably. The dinner party was hosted by a businessman from Stockholm and his wife. Only two other couples besides Jordan and Helmut had been invited. It was touted as a social occasion, but business was the underlying reason for the gathering.

As soon as dinner was concluded in one of the private dining rooms of the Palace Hotel, the group retired to their hosts' suite, where the men sat around a game table and discussed a merger proposition. The women, having nothing in common—not even a language—sat in a small cluster on the formal furniture and tried not to bore each other to death. Jordan had a rudimentary knowledge of German, which the other women spoke, but some of the nuances of the conversation eluded her. It didn't really bother her. Her mind wasn't on the dull conversation anyway.

By the time Helmut finally shook hands all around and prepared to leave, Jordan didn't think she could have stood one more minute in the room. Helmut's varied business pursuits didn't interest her. Strange that she had urged Reeves to talk about his career this afternoon on the ferry. Wanting to share his experiences with him, she had clung to every word.

Now she was bored, tired, cranky—and abysmally miserable whenever she thought about the angry stride with which Reeves had stalked away from her.

She wavered between disappointment and fury. The time they had spent together on the mountaintop and on the ferry had been enchanting. Admittedly, she had regretted that this special day couldn't have carried over into the evening. She couldn't deny that Reeves Grant stirred her, shook her reserve, made her more vulnerable than any other man ever had.

But it was that very susceptibility to him that made him dangerous. Already he was assuming a dominance over her. Hadn't he expected her to break her date with Helmut? At Reeves's whim was she supposed to tell Helmut that she wasn't going to have dinner with him when he had already accepted an invitation on her behalf?

She was angry, but the direction of her anger was hard to pinpoint. Was she angry at Helmut for decreeing a command performance? Or was she mad at Reeves for presuming that he had any right to be possessive of her time? Or was she angry at herself for suddenly becoming a pawn for two very determined, headstrong men— something she had averred she would *never* be again? Not even for love!

In the elevator Helmut expounded upon the pros and cons of the possible merger, and she thought she might very well start screaming if he didn't shut up. What did she care about the business transaction? It meant nothing to her or her life. Up until a few days ago, she had lived tranquilly with very few hurdles in her way. Now it seemed that her world had turned upside down. Nothing was stable anymore. Everything was unclear. Her decisions weren't concrete. Her life had been plunged into chaos ever since the emergence of Reeves Grant into it.

Helmut ushered her out of the elevator as it came to a silent stop on the lobby floor of the hotel. He was helping her with her wrap when she saw the man and woman come through the wide front doors.

The woman was in her mid-twenties, red-haired, svelte, and gorgeous. Her long, slender legs were encased—shockingly so—in tight green satin pants. A loose, blousy sequin top of the same color dipped decidedly low over her pert breasts.

Tacky, Jordan thought. Yes, definitely tacky and taste-less.

Reeves, on the other hand, looked wonderful. He wore gray flannel slacks and a navy blue blazer. His white silk shirt was opened down to the middle of his chest. Black Bally loafers peeked shinily from beneath the crease of his trousers. He was expensively dressed, but with enough casualness to say, I don't give a damn about Old World tradition.

Jordan couldn't help the slight flutter in her throat.

Angry as she was at him, she was more so with herself for responding to his bold sexuality. Even as she admired the well-tailored clothes, she was thinking of the body underneath them and of how it ignited her with consuming flames of passion.

The couple were on their way into the bar when Helmut spotted them. "Reeves," he called across the posh lobby of the famous hotel. "Reeves Grant." Jordan quailed. Vainly she had hoped they could leave without being seen.

Reeves jerked his head around and his face lit up in a disarming smile. "Hello, Helmut, Jordan." He didn't take his arm from its firm position around the redhead's waspish waist. "My favorite subjects. What are you two up to?"

"We were invited to a dinner party," Helmut said.

"Oh, yes." Reeves snapped his fingers. "I remember now you saying something to that effect."

He's lying, Jordan thought. He knew exactly what they were doing here. He hadn't looked her in the eye since Helmut had caught their attention.

"I want you to meet . . . uh . . . Diane? Yes, Diane . . . uh . . . ?"

"Moffett," the woman supplied, and dug into Reeves's ribs with her elbow as though to say, You naughty boy. Jordan clenched her fists. Couldn't the woman stand upright? Must she *recline* against Reeves that way?

"Yes, Diane Moffett," Reeves said, and now he looked at Jordan with a triumphant gleam in his eyes. "Diane, this is Mrs. Jordan Hadlock and Mr. Helmut Eckherdt. Diane's practically a neighbor of mine. She's from Los Angeles. Isn't it lucky we ran into each other this afternoon?"

Jordan couldn't bear to look at his gloating expression any longer and shifted her eyes to the woman, who she thought seemed incredibly stupid. "Hello, Miss Moffett," she said with cold politeness.

"Hi. I like your dress," the woman replied cheekily.

"Thank you." Jordan was glad she had worn this particular dress because she knew it was flattering. It was black sleeveless satin with a ruffled collar that plunged deeply between her breasts. Her waist was cinched with a shocking pink cumberbund. She had pulled her hair into a sleek knot on the back of her neck. Diamond studs in her ears were her only jewelry. Except for Helmut's ring.

"We were on our way to the bar for a nightcap. We'd love for you to join us," Reeves said.

Jordan almost gasped at his audacity. Rage boiled up in her chest until the pressure was painful. The man was totally without morals. How *could* he? How could he pick up another woman so soon after leaving her? Or was that his custom? Out of sight, out of mind? And he had had the gall to play the injured party just a few hours ago!

Helmut turned to her and asked, "Jordan?"

"I really don't think so, Helmut. We've had such a full day, with this morning on the mountain . . ." Her voice trailed off, seemingly with a regretful declination. Actually, the memory of the intimacy she and Reeves had shared in the cable car and at the summit of the mountain had clogged her throat with remorse, and speech was rendered impossible.

"Please excuse us, Reeves, Miss Moffett." Helmut bowed to them. "It seems that my lady is tired. I'd better take her home." He smiled graciously and shook hands with Reeves. He raised the back of Diane Moffett's hand to his lips and kissed it lightly. She giggled.

"Good night then, Helmut, Jordan," Reeves said.

"Good night," Jordan mumbled, and risked looking at him. That was a mistake. His lips were curled derisively and his eyes mocked her. Clearly he was saying, *Coward.*

She raised her chin haughtily as she walked away under the protective guidance of Helmut's arm. But on the inside her heart was breaking. She had been right all along. He was out for thrills. Their night together during the storm had meant no more to him than this redhaired pickup did tonight.

Jordan all but crumpled into the back seat of the limousine and was silent during the ride home. She was amazed at her own absolute despondency. Had this man come to mean so much to her that the idea of him with another woman could reduce her to this stratum of misery?

Even when Helmut escorted her the few remaining blocks through the alleys of the old town, she didn't feel inclined to speak. He attributed her silence to fatigue.

While her lips remained sealed, her mind was working furiously. She argued with herself. She really should tell Helmut now that she didn't intend to marry him. He had asked her earlier in the evening if she had notified her parents yet of their engagement. Evasively, she had reminded him of how busy they had been the past couple of days. He was anxious to make their engagement public.

Somehow, though, she didn't have the energy for such an encounter tonight. He wouldn't take her refusal lying down. There would be arguments to meet, and she didn't think she could manage them. When she felt stronger, when Reeves was banished from her mind, then she would talk to Helmut. Until then . . .

At her door she listlessly endured his good-night embraces. He was a handsome, virile man. His love affairs were legion. Why didn't his mouth excite her? His hands didn't touch her with the same gentle strength that bespoke passion and tenderness at the same time. When he held her, her body didn't seem to fit against his like the second half of a whole.

After he had left her and she was dispiritedly climbing the dark stairs, she chided herself for not feeling more affection for Helmut. He had never shown her anything but kindness. Now he had rescued her from further involvement with an unscrupulous man like Reeves Grant. She should be grateful to Helmut for that. Shouldn't she?

As she got into bed, she tried forcibly to concentrate on Helmut and his generosity. Her brain refused. All she could think of was Reeves with that Diane person and how the silly creature had clung to him. Was he touching her, kissing her? Were his lips whispering those same words he had breathed into her ear as they made love? No! She couldn't bear it. She'd go crazy if she thought of him loving that woman. She'd think of something else.

Her parents. The bookshop. Hot chocolate. Anything. Reeves. Reeves. Reeves.

Just as she was falling asleep, she was marveling at how warm she had felt in the security of his arms despite the misty-gray cold on the top of the mountain.

"Hello," she muttered groggily into the receiver of the telephone. It had rung several times before she realized it wasn't part of her dream. She fumbled for it in the darkness, knocking a book and her alarm clock to the floor before locating it.

"Jordan? Were you asleep?"

"Bill?" She yawned around the name of her supervisor in London. "I . . . yes . . . what time is it?"

"I'm sorry, babe, but I wanted to call and extend my congratulations. Say, baby, this is great news. Someday I want you to tell Uncle Bill how you swung it."

She was wrong. This *was* a dream. She had no idea why her boss would be calling this early in the morning and talking to her so nonsensically. "What are you talking about?" she asked, half into the phone and half into her pillow.

"Come on, Jordan, doll, this is your Bill. I read about your engagement in the *Times*. What a coup. Helmut Eckherdt! When's the big day? Am I invited to the nuptials? I promise to be on my best behavior. I won't get drunk. I won't belch out loud. I won't use crude or abusive language. I won't scratch anything below my waist. I won't—"

"Bill," she interrupted, instantly alert. "Did you say you read about my engagement to Helmut in the *Times*? When?"

"Last night."

Jordan was stunned speechless. "Are you sure? I mean, how can that be?"

"I don't know, baby, but here it is on the third page in black and white. I'm looking at it now and I'm stone sober. There's a two-column article about your romance, complete with a thorough biography of both of you. The writer played up the Cinderella aspect of the story—you know, the beautiful shop girl and the handsome prince angle."

Her mouth was dry and her hands were shaking. "Wh . . . whose by-line is on the piece?"

"James Parker. He's a UPI reporter."

"UPI!" she cried incredulously. The story could feasibly go all over the world, and with Helmut's notoriety, it probably would. "You say the article thoroughly discusses me?"

"In detail, baby. Your childhood, family—you know, the whole schmere."

When Bill had first told her of the article, an inkling of suspicion had flickered in her mind. Now it became full-blown conviction. Who else knew about her background? To whom had she recently revealed the details of her life? Who had prodded her with personal questions, which she had answered unreservedly. Who did she know who was even remotely involved in journalism?

Reeves Grant.

"I have to go, Bill," she said quickly, and bounded out of bed.

"Just a minute, baby. I wanted to tell you not to worry about the newsstand. Your replacement will be arriving in the next few weeks."

"My replacement!" she shrieked, and sank back onto the bed. "My replacement?"

"Well, sure, doll. Somehow I can't see the wife of a billionaire working in a bookstore, can you? You'll be jetting all over the world and—"

"Bill, you don't understand," she said, trying to get a grip on the sanity she felt seeping from her mind. "I'm not marrying Helmut Eckherdt. I'm not marrying any-body."

"But it says right here—"

"I don't give a damn what it says!" she exclaimed angrily. "I'm not marrying him. The story is a mistake. I have been seeing him, but that's all."

"What about a gargantuan diamond engagement ring you're reported to be wearing?"

She sighed and rubbed her forehead with her palm. "I am wearing one, but—"

"Well, then?"

"I . . . It . . . Oh, hell, Bill, it's too hard to explain. Just believe me. I'm not getting married, so you can keep my 'replacement' in London. Now I've got to go—"

"Wait a minute, Jordan." He halted her again. She heard him sigh deeply, ominously, before he said quietly, "Baby, it's not going to be that simple. You see, old man Bauerman has been after me for months to find a job on the Continent for his daughter. She's bored with tea parties and fox hunting and suddenly wants to go to work. Nothing too taxing, you understand—just some-thing to keep her occupied for a while. When I read this article about you last night, I thought your job would be perfect for her. So I called the old man—"

"And gave his daughter my job," she finished for him.

"Well, sort of, yeah."

"Sort of?"

"Well, yeah. She's been promised your job."

A heavy silence hung between them. Jordan was stupefied. What Bill had just told her couldn't be true, yet it was. She had lost her job to Mr. Bauerman's daughter. Mr. Bauerman owned a publishing house as well as the chain of English newsstands she worked for. Things like this happened all the time in the business world. But not to Jordan Hadlock. And it hurt. And it was all Reeves Grant's fault.

"Say, doll, I'm sorry, but—"

"Never mind, Bill. I've got to go now. Call me back later."

Without waiting for his response, she hung up. For long moments she sat on the edge of her bed, her hand still on the receiver of the telephone, willing that everything she had heard over it wasn't true. But it was. An announcement of a wedding that would never take place was going to be plastered on newspapers all over the world. She had been fired from her job.

As she mentally tallied the consequences of Reeves's deceit, a belated fury replaced her bemusement. She balled her fists tightly until her nails made deep half moons in the palms of her hands. "Bastard," she hissed.

She flew off the bed, flinging off her nightgown and rifling through a drawer for a pair of panties. She stepped into them hurriedly and slid on a pair of jeans. She jerked a ski sweater off a hanger in the closet and pulled it on over her head. Her feet were crammed, without the benefit of socks or stockings, into a pair of loafers.

In the bathroom she performed a cursory ablution of face and hands, brushed her teeth, applied a minimum amount of makeup, and haphazardly raked a brush through her thick hair.

Running through her bedroom, she grabbed a jacket and her purse and then dashed down the stairs. She locked the door of the bookstore behind her before quickly turning down the alley into the early-dawn gloom.

Taxis weren't out this early in the morning so she was

forced to reach her destination on foot. She didn't mind. Angry determination was a fuel that propelled her more strongly with each footstep. Her breath frosted on the air, but she was untouched by the cold as she marched through the streets of Lucerne.

The row of hotels across the street from the lake was quiet and still. The wide verandas that fronted most of them were empty of loungers who could be found there later in the day, sipping drinks and taking in the scenery.

The lobby of the Europa was vacant except for two maids who were polishing mirrors and dusting furniture. The concierge was sorting through registry cards when she strode toward the desk and planted her hands flat on the smooth marble surface of the countertop.

"What room is Mr. Reeves Grant in?" she demanded.

The concierge raised his eyebrows in query and studied her disheveled appearance. "I beg your pardon?" he asked in accented English.

His wariness cautioned Jordan and she made herself smile beguilingly. "I know I must look a fright, but I've been driving all night to surprise him. He's my . . . friend," she added with deliberate insinuation. "You understand, don't you?" Her eyelashes batted down over the fiery gray eyes and the man was helpless.

"Y . . . Yes, of course. He . . . uh . . . let's see now. Room four twenty-nine. Shall I ring him?"

"No!" she said quickly. Then she ducked her head shyly and swallowed her disgust. "I want to surprise him."

The concierge grinned lustily. He was a true romantic. "The elevators are to your right," he whispered, as though they were conspirators.

"Thank you," she said over her shoulder, for she was

already crossing the lobby with hurried footsteps. After what must be the slowest elevator in the world finally ground to a halt, she stepped into it and pressed the button for the fourth floor. As it ascended, she rehearsed the aspersions she was going to heap on him.

When the doors slid open, she barged out and stormed down the hallway, realized she was going the wrong way, spun around, and struck off in the opposite direction until she stood outside his room.

Her knock was none too gentle. It echoed down the long narrow corridor. She'd be lucky if no one else peeked out their door to see who was behaving with such noisy rudeness so early in the morning.

The occupant of Room 429 hadn't stirred, so she knocked again with more emphasis. There was a rustling of covers and suddenly Jordan realized that he might not be alone. Her heart lurched sickly at that thought, but she stubbornly raised her chin. She had come to tell him just what she thought of him, and she didn't care if she had an audience.

Resolution made her next knock on the heavy wooden door thunderous. This time she heard a mumbled curse and the squeaking of a mattress. Soft footsteps brought him to the other side of the door.

"Yes?" It was more a belligerent growl than a word.

"Open the door," was all she said.

There was a momentary hesitation, then she heard the lock being flipped up and the door swung open. He was standing behind it, out of sight.

She pushed past the door, her eyes going immediately to the bed. They found it empty, and she breathed a sigh of relief. Her back was rigid as she stamped further into the room.

"Come in," he said drily from behind her.

She swiveled around and confronted him, armed with righteous indignation and intent on dressing him down until he begged for forgiveness.

But Reeves didn't fight fair. He was naked.

Tousled strands of mahogany-colored hair hung on his forehead. His hands were planted firmly on his hips in an arrogant pose. To a woman who was fighting for her life as well as combating a strong attraction to the man, he was a formidable foe.

She hadn't considered that she might find him this way. She knew he would probably be asleep, but she hadn't thought beyond that. Now her motivation drained from her under the destructive force of his arresting masculinity. The hair on his chest grew in a mesmerizing pattern that she traced with her eyes. It tapered to a thin silky line that disappeared into . . .

His legs were long and lean and hard. He exuded virile power. What a frail exercise her attack would be. How could she possibly win? To him she must appear foolish, charging in as she had done.

Even as she glared at him, he yawned broadly and politely covered it with his hand. That insouciance angered her as nothing else had and her rage came back in full force. But before she had a chance to vent it, he said, "Don't you think you're being rather forward? Didn't your mother ever tell you that men like to be the aggressors?"

"Damn you!" she threw at him. "How could you do such a despicable thing? Never in my life have I known anyone with less sensitivity."

He stared at her a moment with something akin to

amusement lighting his green eyes. He walked past her, picked up his wristwatch from the bedside table, checked the time, and then sat down on the edge of the bed. "What could I have possibly done this early in the day to make you so angry?"

"Oh, please, spare me the innocent act. You know what you've done. Your deceit is surpassed only by your grasping ambition. I spilled my whole life story to you—" As she launched into her tirade, he leaned back against the pillows and raised one knee, resting a dangling hand on it. She averted her eyes quickly and asked unsteadily, "Would you please put some . . . clothes on?"

"No."

She whirled her head back to him. "You're wretched."

"I?" he asked. "I? You're the one who came barging into my bedroom at this ungodly hour. You routed me out of bed. I don't sleep in my clothes. This is the way you found me, and I don't feel inclined to dress at the moment."

"You're indecent."

His eyes toured her figure and a lewd grin spread across his face. "So is what I'm thinking."

She gritted her teeth, but wouldn't give him the satisfaction of honoring his provocative words. Willing her eyes away from his nakedness, she restructured her thoughts and asked, "Do you know a man named James Parker?"

He seemed surprised by her question, but he answered promptly. "Yes. He's a reporter for UPI out of the London bureau."

"And you called him yesterday and told him all about Helmut and me. The fruits of your labor are smeared on the third page of last evening's *Times*. If my shop were open on Sundays, I'd sell you a copy," she said scathingly.

He shook his head and wearily ran a hand through his hair. "Jordan, I don't—"

"You deliberately urged me to talk about myself yesterday, prying into my private life and its history. You put on a good act, Mr. Grant. I never suspected that you were only doing your research."

"Jordan—"

"I would have much preferred that you tell me what you were doing. I might have even been cooperative. You needn't have wooed me with kisses. Or is that the way you do your best work? Mixing business with pleasure?" To her chagrin, tears formed deep pools in her eyes and blurred her vision. Furiously she wiped them away.

He held up his hand to halt her next words. "Let me get this straight," he said calmly. "Jim wrote a story for the *Times* about you and Helmut and your engagement, and you think that I leaked it to him?"

"You did!"

"No I didn't, Jordan."

"You had to have," she shouted. "Don't compound my loathing for you with more lies. I'm sick to death of your duplicity."

He sprang off the bed and had her arms imprisoned by iron hands before she could blink. "Don't lecture me about duplicity," he said through his teeth. "You know what duplicity is? Duplicity is a woman who snuggles and cuddles one man while being engaged to another. And all the while she claims to the poor sucker she's cuddling that said engagement isn't real. Don't accuse me of playacting, Jordan. You could give Sarah Bernhardt lessons."

She tried to extricate herself from his tenacious hold, but her efforts didn't even serve to loosen it. "I'm *not* engaged to Helmut. You know that."

"Do I? You say you aren't committed to him, yet every time he crooks his finger you go running after him. That sounds pretty permanent to me."

"I don't want to hurt him," she cried. "I want to be fair. But you wouldn't know about fair play, would you? You play to win. You play for blood, and you don't care who bleeds. All you want is a good time and a good photograph and a good story."

He lifted her off the floor, twirled her around, and tossed her onto the bed. He followed with his own body stretched down the length of hers. His hands pinned her arms to either side of her head.

"I didn't leak that damned story," he said with emphasis on each word as his hands dug more deeply into the flesh of her wrists. "I didn't." He gave her a little shake.

Her eyes were wide with fear and disbelief, but he met them levelly. She wet her dry lips with her tongue before asking, "Then who—"

"It could have been anyone. There were fifty or sixty people there the other night when you so naively asked them not to tell anyone about your engagement. That set thrives on gossip, Jordan. They could have tipped off any dozen hungry reporters." His hands holding her wrists were inescapable, but the truth that radiated from his eyes held her in a tighter bondage. She squeezed her own eyes shut.

"But Bill said that the writer knew so much about me," she argued. "Yesterday—"

"Doesn't Helmut know all of that, too? Haven't you told him bits and pieces of your history? He could have passed them along. And so on and so on, until a gifted reporter could have built a comprehensive story around them."

Jordan thought back over the last few months. She supposed what Reeves said had credence. Was he telling her the truth?

As though reading her thoughts, he said, "I'll admit to being as mad as hell yesterday when we got off that boat. And I know that the evidence against me is incriminating. If I had done it, I'd take the credit—or blame, as it were. But I didn't do it, Jordan. I swear it."

She opened her eyes then and was awed at how green his were this close up. The freckles that seemed to appear and disappear at will were so close she could count them. "Did you sleep with that girl last night?" The question caught them both off guard. Jordan hadn't intended to ask it. It had just slipped out.

For a moment Reeves looked puzzled, then he shook his head and laughed softly. "That dimwit?" he asked scornfully. "I haven't lived a celibate life for thirty-five years, but give me some credit, Jordan," he chuckled. "I picked her up here in the bar and hustled her over to the Palace. Helmut had mentioned after our meeting in his offices that that's where the dinner party was going to be. As soon as you left, I dumped her. I've never heard such foul language come out of a woman's mouth."

"Why would you go to so much trouble?" At some point her hands had been released and were now examining that intriguing growth pattern of hair on his chest.

He shifted his body over hers and ducked his head.

"Why do you think?" he asked against her ear. His lips stayed to tease the sensitive lobe.

"Because you wanted to make someone jealous?" she asked timidly.

"You got it."

"Oh, Reeves," she sighed. "I came here ready to scratch your eyes out and now . . ." Her voice trailed away under the maneuvering of his mouth on her neck. "You're too quick for me. I can never keep up with you. You make me angry, then leave me bewildered. You're like no other man I've ever met. What am I going to do with you?"

He raised his head and peered at her suggestively. "I have an idea," he drawled.

"No!" she exclaimed, and tried to push him off. When she realized the futility of that, she tossed her head from side to side, but his mouth chased her relentlessly. "Reeves, what happened with us before—"

"Defies description."

"Yes . . . I mean no. It was wrong. I don't know how I . . ." His mouth had caught up to hers now and was teasing it with small kisses in the corners. She tried to talk around it. "I . . . We can't . . . We mustn't . . ."

"Yes we can. Yes we must."

"No. I don't want to."

"And you're a liar. Liar." He finally tired of the foolishness and closed his mouth over hers, trapping inside any words of affected protest.

Their mouths met with a hunger too long denied. The tip of his tongue flicked over her parted lips, tormenting them mercilessly before pushing past them into her mouth and sampling its delights.

She wasn't idly submissive. Her lips closed around his

tongue, entrapping it tightly, until he was moaning his pleasure. When at last he pulled away, it was only to allow them to breathe. She turned her head onto his pillow as his lips journeyed over her neck to her ear and paid it homage.

"Reeves," she whispered. "I love this bed."

"Why?"

"Because it's still warm from your body. It smells like you."

"Oh, God," he grated.

He wrapped his arms around her and rolled her over until she lay atop him. With eager hands he peeled off her jacket. He found the bottom of her sweater and worked it over her stomach and breasts and shoulders, then pulled it over her head. Laughing with him, she disengaged her arms from the sleeves.

He flung the offending garment aside, riveting his eyes on her breasts, which were offered to him so enticingly. His fingertips grazed over the top curves with an almost reverent touch. "Beautiful breasts." His voice was low and deep. His hands slipped to the undersides and cupped her, lifting her, enjoying the full plumpness that filled her. His thumbs gently skimmed across the dusky pink nipples. "I love to watch that," he said when they puckered prettily.

Jordan arched her back and gasped her pleasure. One hand clamped her around the neck and pulled her face down to his. Hotly, his lips sipped at hers while his other hand stayed at her breast to coax responses from it that left her breathless.

At first, she thought the sinking feeling came from the intoxicating kiss, but she realized that he was easing her onto her back once again.

When her head was nestled on his pillow, his mouth left hers and nibbled its way down her neck and chest. Her nipple disappeared between his lips. By gently flexing his cheeks, he fed on her sweetness. His tongue became a darting, flicking instrument of sensuality that brought her to a level of arousal she had never known before.

She trembled beneath him.

"Jordan. I want you. I've wanted you since I left your apartment early that morning after the storm. The hardest thing I've ever done in my life was to leave you in that bed. God, I wanted you so bad yesterday I hurt."

He raised himself until his face was hovering over hers. His eyes never left hers as he gently nudged her knees apart and settled himself between her thighs. They fit together with a cohesion so unique that it was awesome.

"Feel how right it is," he whispered urgently.

"Yes," she said, and moved against that hard strength that declared his need.

"Ah, Jordan, Jordan . . . take me inside you."

His lips came down on hers possessively. The metallic whisper of a zipper was the only sound in the room as he worked at the fastening of her jeans. Then his hand was sliding leisurely over her stomach, past her navel, and finally beneath the lacy band of her bikini panties. Satin skin. A downy tuft. Then . . .

He sighed. "So soft. So female. I need you, Jordan. And you need me. Now."

Then he touched her with startling accuracy and involuntarily she closed around his stroking fingers, groaning her acquiescence. "Yes, Reeves. Now."

"Jordan, you must know—"

The shrill ring of the telephone cut off his words.

117

7

Reeves cursed expansively when the telephone rang a second and then a third time. They froze, staring at each other. She smiled with sad resignation. He eased himself away from her and jerked the receiver from the ringing telephone.

"Grant," he barked. His eyes swung to her as the caller identified himself. Reeves said, "Hello, Helmut."

Jordan covered her face with her hands and rolled over onto her side. A tiny sob was the only sound she made.

"No, you didn't awaken me," Reeves said. "I was up."

The double entendre didn't escape her. Nor was it meant to. The scornful tone in his voice was intentional.

She sat up and scooted to the other side of the bed, hastily picking up her sweater and pulling it on. Without looking back at Reeves, she refastened her jeans and smoothed trembling, ineffectual hands over her hair.

Reeves listened to Helmut. Jordan walked to the window and stared out unseeingly at the lake water, which now sparkled in the first sunlight. She clutched the pull cord of the drape when she heard Reeves ask, "Have you tried to reach Jordan?"

She whirled around and met his steely gaze from across the room. He was holding the telephone at his ear, pausing, silently asking her what he should say next. One look at her shattered face and he knew. In the depths of her gray eyes he saw her plea for him not to tell Helmut she was there. His lips hardened into a bitter line, but his voice remained cool as he answered, "No, she probably isn't awake yet."

He listened while he stared at Jordan, where she stood immobile at the window. "That sounds great. Where should I meet you? . . . All right . . . an hour is fine. . . . Yes. See you then."

Long after Helmut had broken the connection, Reeves held the telephone to his ear, piercing Jordan with his implacable stare. Then he juggled the receiver from one hand to the other and replaced it.

He leaned down and scooped her jacket from the floor, then stood up and went to the door. He stood there with one hand on his hip, the other extended, holding her jacket toward her.

She took the less-than-subtle hint. With false bravado,

she lifted her chin and stalked toward him. When she was within a few feet of the door, he threw the jacket toward her so forcefully that her hands had to come up quickly and grasp it.

"Your fiancé," he said slurringly, "wants to go hiking on the mountain today. I suggest that you scuttle home like a good little girl and await his call, which will come in about twenty minutes. Always a true gentleman, he is allowing you an extra few minutes of sleep."

The mockery in his voice was wounding, and, reflexively, she flinched under it. He wasn't finished yet.

"I'll see you in about an hour. We're to converge here on the porch of the hotel." She walked past him. When her hand was on the door knob, he added, "Remember to sound sleepy and surprised when he calls."

She shot him a withering look and then flung the door open. She almost made it into the hall before he grabbed her elbow and swung her around. "As for waking me up, you beat a cup of coffee all to hell, Jordan." The scathing insult dripped with disdain. Before she could respond to it, he shoved her through the door and slammed it behind her.

She didn't waste any time returning home. The obliging concierge was busy with a guest who was checking out, so he didn't see her as she skirted past his desk and out of the hotel.

Breathless and humiliated, she reached home just as the telephone started ringing. Reeves's words came back to haunt her as she picked up the phone and answered brightly, "Good morning."

"Darling, are you up and about?" Helmut asked.

It gave her a sense of relief and salved her conscience

to answer truthfully rather than to lie to him. "Yes, I've been up for a long while. Bill called this morning," she added.

"I have an idea," Helmut said, and invited her on the hiking expedition.

"That sounds great," she enthused.

"That's exactly what Reeves said."

Oh, God. Had it been? Yes. He had said those exact words.

"Can you be ready by nine?" Helmut asked. "I told Reeves we would all meet at the Europa. Do you mind too terribly going there alone?"

In light of the fact that she had already walked through the gray shadows of predawn to the hotel, she almost succumbed to the hysterical laughter she felt building in her chest. "No, not at all," she answered with amazing calm.

"I'll see you then, darling." He hung up with his usual abruptness.

Mechanically, she dressed. She kept on the jeans she was already wearing, but tucked them into the hiking boots she had purchased soon after coming to Lucerne. Hiking in the foothills was a popular pastime.

She went into the bathroom and whipped the ski sweater over her head. Her breasts were chafed in spots where Reeves's whisker stubble had abraded her. At seeing them she tried to conjure up angry resentment. Instead, to her shame, her insides melted and liquified at the recollection of his kisses. Actually she thrilled to this raw evidence of his masculine aggression.

Her face bore further traces of his lovemaking. Her lips had that full, pouting, well-kissed look. What small amount of makeup she had applied to her eyes earlier had been smudged by their turbulent kisses. Hastily she cleaned her face and began again.

When she was done, she swept her hair into a ponytail. Determinedly she put on a bra, a shirt with a button-down collar, and a V-necked navy-blue sweater. Nothing about her attire connoted femininity. That was paramount in her choice of wardrobe.

Since the day promised to be clear and warm, she left her fur parka behind and took a flannel-lined khaki poplin jacket. After stuffing some grooming articles in a backpack, she was ready.

Traffic had picked up on the streets now as she walked to the hotel. Helmut and Reeves were waiting for her on the porch, sitting in the comfortable chairs and sipping coffee.

Warily her eyes sifted over Reeves as Helmut embraced her with conditioned familiarity. She mumbled a good morning and skittishly stepped away from him.

"You're angry with me." Helmut's unexpected sentence wasn't a question.

"What?" she asked in bewilderment.

"Our engagement. The secret is out, my darling. It's in newspapers all over the Continent, maybe America, too. I'm sorry. Apparently one of my guests couldn't keep a secret." He took her hand conciliatorily.

She risked looking at Reeves, but he was engrossed in cleaning one of his lenses with more thoroughness than it warranted. "I—"

"I hope you aren't too angry," Helmut interrupted her. "For myself, I'm delighted that the world knows you belong to me."

His chauvinistic declaration of possession rankled, but

she didn't want to cause a scene with Reeves sitting right there, so she said, "Well, anyway, the damage is done."

Helmut turned her hand over and kissed the palm. When he straightened he asked, "Would you like some breakfast, my dear? You have plenty of time. The hotel's kitchen is packing us a picnic lunch."

"Just some chocolate and a croissant, please," she said as she stowed her backpack in the chair next to Reeves and settled herself in another.

While she nibbled at her breakfast, the two men ignored her and debated the pros and cons of OPEC's latest oil price increase. She took the unguarded opportunity to look at Reeves. He was wearing a pair of lederhosen. Over the gray suede shorts, he had on a white cable-knit sweater. He even wore dark green knee socks that matched the leather trim on the shorts and brown suede hiking boots with red laces. A bright yellow wind breaker lay across his camera case. He was ruggedly handsome. The morning breeze off the lake stirred the dark hair with its russet highlights shining in the sunlight. He squinted against the shimmering water of the lake and his eyes were screened by thick, curled lashes.

Absently he tugged on his earlobe as he listened carefully to what Helmut was saying. It came to her quite unexpectedly then that she loved him.

It wasn't possible, of course. Men as vital and attractive as Reeves existed only in the movies. They didn't stumble into the lives of shopkeepers. But he had. Only he hadn't stumbled. He had been thrust into her life with the impetus of a thunderstorm. She realized now as she continued watching him that she had loved him from the first moment she had seen him. Otherwise she couldn't have done what she had that night.

Sleeping with him was no casual thing for her. She had done it out of an emotion she now recognized as love. Had Helmut not called this morning, she might very well be in Reeves's bed this minute.

But for Reeves it was different. He was motivated by no such emotion. He found her attractive, yes. And he wanted to make love to her, yes. But when he left Lucerne for his next project, she would soon be replaced by another woman in another town, another country, another continent.

Jordan wasn't disillusioned. Balloons, beautiful as they were, burst easily. Sand castles were swept away with the tide. Reeves would leave her and then where would she be? Without Helmut, for she must tell him soon that she wouldn't marry him. Without a job. Bill, as much as he liked her, would look after his own security in Mr. Bauerman's favor.

Without Reeves.

Hot, prickly tears stung her eyes and she turned her head toward the lake, where the bright sunlight reflecting on the water would provide an excuse for her streaming eyes should anyone notice them. She couldn't let Reeves know. Steeling herself against him would be difficult if not impossible, but she must do it. He couldn't ever guess how she felt. In reminiscence, he could tell his buddies that she had been attractive, that she had been "easy," but he would never be able to tell them that she had been a fool.

She jumped guiltily when Helmut spoke her name. "Are you finished?" he asked, indicating the now cold roll and chocolate.

"Y . . . yes. I guess I wasn't very hungry."

"Then let's be off." Helmut picked up the basket that one of the hotel's staff had brought out to him and led them down the steep steps toward the waiting limousine.

"Jordan, you haven't commented on Reeves's costume. He looks like one of us natives, doesn't he?" Helmut asked.

She looked at Reeves as if noticing him for the first time. "Yes, he does," she said brightly.

Reeves grinned. "I went shopping yesterday and came away with these." He indicated the lederhosen. "I only hope my knees don't get cold." His smile was so boyish that Jordan's heart swelled and she forgot the resolution she had so recently made.

She looked down at the long, lean legs with their rock-hard muscles. His knees were sprinkled with dark, springy hair. She remembered kissing them on that rain-drenched night they had spent together. She had been kneeling beside him leaning over. Her hair had swept across his thighs. He had caught the silky skein in his hand and told her how good it felt against his skin. Her cheek had rested on his thigh.

Unbearable heat bathed her body as she raised her eyes to Reeves's face. He must have been remembering the same incident, for his eyes fairly smoldered with green fire. The hostility of that morning dissolved and they smiled at each other with recollection of a shared secret.

Then, as Reeves watched, the radiant glow in Jordan's eyes dimmed. Her smile diminished to a sad grimace, then vanished altogether. She turned away quickly.

His camera case, her backpack, and the picnic basket were placed in the trunk of the car and they got into the back seat. Henri let them out at a convenient spot where there was a gradual grassy incline into the foothills. "It's not too arduous," Helmut said, smiling genially.

Indeed it wasn't, even loaded down as they were with their cargo. Families with small children trooped up the hill, enjoying the Sunday outing. Sweethearts, more interested in each other than in vigorous exercise, strolled with arms around each other's waists up the hill. A group of adolescent boys was playing with a soccer ball. One would kick it up the incline several yards. When it rolled back down, another would kick it, and so on. It looked like an exhausting effort and Helmut said as much.

They climbed, resting periodically, for about two hours until they reached a plateau at the timberline and decided that it was an ideal place to spread their lunch. Helmut had brought a blanket from the trunk of his car and now spread it out on the grass that was already losing some of its verdure due to the lateness of the season.

Jordan eased off her backpack and set it on the ground. Reeves deposited his camera case nearby after first taking out the Nikon. He plopped down on the blanket, but not in a relaxing posture. Instead he began snapping pictures of Jordan and Helmut with the mountain scenery in the background.

They rested for a while, chatting and teasing each other about their lack of physical prowess and stamina, before Jordan began unloading the picnic basket. She was swatting away two pairs of impatient hands that pilfered the dishes as soon as she uncovered them when two young men raced up toward them. They were both dressed in jogging shorts and tank tops. They were wearing hiking boots, which seemed incongruous to their runner's garb.

One of them heaved a deep breath and asked Helmut in German, "Are you Mr. Eckherdt?"

Helmut sat up from his half-reclining position and answered affirmatively. The young man reached into the waistband of his shorts and extracted an envelope that was now somewhat soggy with healthy perspiration.

At Helmut's quizzical expression the young man rushed to explain. "Your chauffeur gave me this to bring to you. I'm a marathon runner in training. When he saw I was going to run up here, he asked me to find you and give you this message." He looked toward his companion, who nodded in agreement.

"Thank you," Helmut said, and dug in the pocket of his pants. As he shook hands with the young men, he pressed a bank note into each of their palms.

"Danke schön," they chorused before starting off again.

Helmut opened the envelope and read the brief message. He cursed under his breath. "Forgive me, both of you, but I must return to town. One of our company airplanes is missing somewhere over Canada. I must be on hand when word comes in."

"Of course," Jordan said, and hastily began placing the food back into the basket.

Helmut grabbed both her hands and stayed them. "No, Jordan. I feel badly enough as it is. I won't spoil your day, too. You and Reeves stay and enjoy the picnic."

"But, Helmut—" She started to object.

"There's nothing either of you can do, darling. Nor can I, really. But I must be there in case the worst conjecture proves to be correct."

"But—"

"I insist. Reeves, enjoy the day. I wish I didn't have to desert you this way. Damn."

"Don't apologize, Helmut. I only hope that your airplane and its crew are found to be safe."

"As do I," Jordan murmured.

Helmut kissed her softly on the mouth and said, "I'll try to call you later this evening, darling, if I can."

"I'll see that the basket is returned to the Europa and that Jordan gets home," Reeves said.

"Thank you, my friend." Helmut, thinking of business now, turned and jogged down the hill, then disappeared behind some towering pines.

Jordan stared after the retreating figure, aware that she was once again alone with Reeves on what should be an idyllic outing. Reeves was aware of their isolation, too. The tension between them was palpable. She was afraid to meet his eyes, not able to guess what his mood might be. He ended the suspense.

"Well, get busy, woman. I'm starving," he said, and flipped back the cover of the basket again.

"Haven't you heard of women's liberation?" she snapped.

"Yeah. Whose rotten idea was that?" he scowled.

In the long run he helped her unload the basket. To their delight, Helmut's idea of a picnic was ludicrous. Silver lids capped glass jars of pâté, caviar, smoked salmon, and smoked oysters. A cold baked chicken had been rid of bones and trimmed of fat. There was a selection of relishes, including pickles, olives, deviled eggs, and preserved fruit. Several loaves of bread, the crusts hard and golden, the centers soft and white, were wrapped in linen towels. Whole cheeses and a crock of

butter were still cool. A box of chocolates and a selection
of pastries were included for dessert. A bottle of white
German wine, a bottle of cognac, and a thermos of coffee
had been secured to the side of the basket so they would
stand upright. China plates, linen napkins, and silver
cutlery were packed into the bottom of the hamper.

"My God," Reeves exclaimed. "Who did he expect to
feed?"

"What I can't figure out is how he carried it all up here.
I had no idea how heavy that basket was. Did you?"

"No. I'm only glad he didn't ask me to help him!"

They ate until they couldn't hold any more. They
drank most of the wine, but Jordan suggested that
Reeves replace the cork rather than try to drink it all or
they might have to stagger down the hill. She demolished
the box of Swiss chocolates. He ate two of the pastries,
licking the rich fillings off his fingers.

They had barely made a dent in all the food, so they
conscientiously repacked the remains in the hamper.
When that task was done, Jordan stood up and stretched.
"I've got to walk some of this off."

"Good idea," he said. "I wanted to go a little higher
anyway."

"Who's going to carry the basket?" she asked.

He frowned down at it, knowing that their lunch hadn't
appreciably lightened the basket. "I'll make a deal with
you," he offered. "If you can get the camera case, I'll
take the basket."

"All right," she said.

"Are you sure? It's pretty heavy."

"Well, the backpack isn't. I don't think I'll have any
problem."

When they were loaded and their gear was adjusted comfortably, they began walking higher up the mountain. The grass gave way to rockier ground, though they were still in the timberline and the incline wasn't steep. Other hikers were still in evidence, though most had stayed on the plateaus below.

"Have you ever done any serious mountain climbing, Reeves?" she asked breathlessly as she clambered along beside him.

"Are you kidding?" He shot her a dark look.

She laughed. "Oh, yes. I forgot about your acrophobia."

"Anyone who hangs off the side of a mountain for no good reason is crazy."

"But this doesn't bother you," she pointed out.

"No. This isn't like hanging by ropes and finding footholds and . . . God, I get goose bumps just thinking about it."

"You may be getting goose bumps because it's getting colder," she observed. "I think I'll put my jacket on." She set his camera case down on a level rock and eased off her backpack. Taking her jacket out of it, she shrugged into it. "Aren't you going to put on your windbreaker?"

"No. This sweater is like a furnace. I'm still warm."

They went on, going higher and talking less to save their breath, which was becoming more labored the higher they got.

"I . . . think . . . I'm going to have . . . to . . . rest," she said between rapid pants.

"Good idea," he concurred, and virtually collapsed on the ground under a pine tree. "Actually, I was ready to stop about twenty minutes ago, but my macho image would have been irreparably damaged had I cried uncle before you."

"It would take more than that to jeopardize your machismo."

The minute the words left her lips she wished she could recall them. They were all but an admission as to how much he attracted her. She blushed furiously when he cocked an eyebrow at her. "Oh, yeah?" he taunted. "Tell me all about it."

"Not on your life," she said sourly. "You're too conceited as it is."

Still grinning and not in the least affected by her acerbic tone, he got up and took the blanket out of the basket and spread it under the tree. "Let's rest before starting back."

She sat down and leaned against the tree trunk, sighing tiredly but contentedly. He didn't ask her permission before lying down on his back and settling his head on her lap. "Good night," he said, shutting his eyes.

She cleared her throat loudly. "Mr. Grant." He opened one eye and looked up at her through the forest of lashes. "Who thought up the sleeping arrangements?" she asked.

"I'm entitled to the most comfortable position. I had to carry the heaviest load," he reasoned.

"But you're stronger. You're a man and I'm a woman."

"I noticed that," he said lazily as his eyes dropped significantly to her breasts.

Hurriedly getting back on the subject, she said, "I have to take two steps to your one. Your legs are longer."

"Yours are smoother. And shapelier." He reached

behind his head, slid his hand under the denim, and captured her relaxed calf in his hand. Immediately the delicate muscles beneath his fingers contracted. "As a matter of fact," he continued soothingly, "you're smooth and shapely all over."

Her head began pounding with her accelerated pulse. She looked away quickly, then, unable to resist the temptation, back down at him as he grinned up at her.

"My anatomy is not a proper subject for discussion," she said primly.

"I think it is. Since you opened the door to me the other night and invited me in out of the rain, your anatomy has been the only subject my mind has been capable of dwelling on."

"That's unhealthy."

"Uh-huh. You make me feel very healthy. Very strong. Sometimes embarrassingly so."

She caught her bottom lip between her teeth and looked away again. Don't let him talk to you like this, she commissioned herself. Get up. Move away. Run. But then he laughed and captured her hand, kissing the palm quickly, then with more leisure. Thoughts of resistance or escape dissolved under the soft, moist persuasions of his mouth.

Looking down at him as he nibbled the frail bones of her wrist, she was again suffused with love. "Reeves?" she whispered.

The soft tone of her voice was more attention-getting than if she had shouted at him. "Yes?" he asked, looking up at her.

"I couldn't let you tell Helmut that I was in your room with you. You understand that, don't you?"

He sighed and muttered an expletive. "Yes. At the time I was furious, but . . ." He stared off in the distance for a long moment, then looked back up at her. "The guy just called me his friend a while ago." It was a small concession. He was telling her that he understood the loyalty she felt. He shifted his weight and rose up on one elbow to face her. "Jordan, just for today, let's not talk about Helmut. All right?"

"Reeves—"

"Please? Just for today. Tomorrow will take care of itself."

That was so easy for him to say. He was able to pack his bags and leave. No guilt, no remorse, no regrets. While she . . .

It was the mute appeal in his eyes she couldn't resist. "All right," she heard herself say aloud while answers to the contrary paraded through her mind.

He reached up behind her head and pulled out the barette that held her ponytail. Released, her hair fell about her face and neck. He smiled and lay his head again in her lap. "Kiss me," he said.

The die was cast.

Jordan didn't think of refusing. Instead, she leaned over him and pressed her lips to his. He didn't move. Neither accepting nor rejecting her kiss, he just lay there. He was issuing a challenge she wasn't about to ignore.

Her hand moved down the hard wall of his chest until it insinuated its way under the heavy sweater. It brushed past the waist band of his shorts to caress the warm, vibrant skin. She fanned the crinkly hair on his chest before settling her palm over the masculine contours and massaging them.

Her lips parted slightly and treated his face to kisses so light he might well have imagined them. With his eyes closed, he couldn't tell where the next feather-light touch would strike. She kissed him at the temple, on the eyebrows, the eyelids, the nose, the hard cheek, and the rigid line of jaw. But she moved out of order, with no sequence, so that each kiss was an unexpected gift. Eventually she worked her way back to his mouth. She saw his lips form her name.

Her tongue, warm and wet, stroked along his bottom lip and urged the corners of his mouth to relax. At the same time, her fingertips found that hard kernel of flesh on his chest nestled in the soft mat of hair and worried it until it became distended. He groaned softly while she played with it as her tongue demanded entrance to his mouth.

At last he relented. Violently. He crooked his outside arm around her neck and drew her closer. His head maneuvered between her breasts and his mouth allowed her tongue its sweet violation.

"You taste like chocolate," he breathed between kisses.

"I'm sorry."

"I love it. You're delicious."

"So are you."

They kissed again while her hand traced the silky line of hair that disappeared into the waistband of his shorts. She explored his navel.

"Do you know what that's doing to me?" he grated.

Suddenly she did know and was shocked at what she was doing. She yanked her hand from under his sweater and sat erect, smoothing her hair. Her breath was erratic. It matched his.

"I wasn't complaining, you know." His eyes were twinkling mischievously.

"Yes, I know. I didn't realize . . . It's . . . I . . ." She was confused by her own unstable emotions and the throbbing ache deep in her body that begged cessation.

He caught her hand to his chest as he folded his arms across it. "Let's take a nap. Then we can start back down."

"All right."

She sighed and leaned her head back against the rough bark of the tree, but for some reason, she wasn't uncomfortable. Her contentment had something to do with the heavy weight of his head on her thighs and abdomen, with the warm, moist breath she could feel on her stomach through her clothes, and with the even beating of the heart that pumped strong and sure beneath her hand.

She took one last look at Reeves, then closed her eyes. Within seconds her breath was synchronized with his and they both slept.

It wasn't a sound that awakened her. Rather it was the pervading silence. She opened her eyes slowly, trying to assimilate where she was. Her sleep had been deep and reviving, but it seemed that she was trapped in a wakeful dream.

She and Reeves were under the protective branches of the pine, but the rest of the world, outside the perimeter of the wide, spreading limbs, was dusted with white talc. It looked like a fairyland of swirling white crystals.

Even as she glanced down at Reeves, one of the

crystals filtered through the pine needles and settled on his eyelashes.

Jordan raised her head and stared out at the scene once again. Sudden clarity rang loud alarms in her head. This wasn't a dream.

"Reeves," she cried, shaking him awake. "It's snowing!"

8

~~~~~~~~~~~~~~~~~~

hat?" He sat up so abruptly that they almost bumped heads. "My God! Will you look at that!" He came to his feet and spread his arms wide to catch the snowflakes that danced around them.

"What are we going to do?" Jordan asked anxiously.

"Do? What do you mean do?"

"Reeves, we're up here on this mountain in a snowstorm. How will we get down?"

He smiled and hugged her briefly. "The same way we came up. It doesn't look too bad. If we hurry, we'll be fine. Does it usually snow this early in the season?"

She was looking at the snowfall, still not convinced that their trip back down the mountain wouldn't be dangerous. "Sometimes up here in the higher elevations it does. It's probably not even snowing in the valley."

"We may walk out of it in a short while then. Come on, let's get started." He sounded calm and assured that they really weren't in a predicament, but Jordan saw him eyeing the snow and calculating how quickly it was coming down. The wind was blowing harder now and the temperature seemed to be dropping each minute. Already a sheet of white coated the ground.

Hurriedly, without speaking, they gathered up their things. Jordan hauled the camera case over her shoulder after remounting the backpack on her back. Reeves draped the blanket that had served as their picnic table over her head and shoulders. "Just in case you can't take the cold." He cuffed her under the chin and winked. He was trying to keep her from panicking, but she was still cautious and worried as they stepped from under the protective limbs of the tree and the full force of the storm hit them.

She let Reeves navigate. He plunged ahead and she trailed him as closely as her stumbling footsteps would allow her to. Every few yards he would glance over his shoulder to see that she was behind him. The wind ripped attempted words from their mouths, so they communicated with an improvised sign language.

Usually walking down the mountain trail wasn't difficult at all. Now, however, the path was obscured by the first layer of snow. It had already frozen hard in patches and walking over them was treacherous. The wind lashed at their faces and stung their eyes, making it difficult for them to see.

Reeves waved for her to follow him under another pine that offered a modicum of protection. "Do you think we're going in the right direction?" he shouted.

Jordan quaked at his question. She had been following his lead, not really paying attention to where they were going, concentrating only on putting one foot in front of the other and trying not to fall down on the icy ground underfoot.

"I don't know, Reeves. I think so, but . . ."

She looked up at him so fearfully that he hugged her to him and said, "Hey, now, don't worry. I'm going to get us out of this. Are you cold?"

"No," she lied. She couldn't complain about being cold when she was wrapped in the blanket and he only had on the thin windbreaker over his sweater. Only knee socks covered the lower half of his legs.

"Ready?" he asked. She nodded. "Tell me if you need to stop again." She nodded again and then followed him back into the storm.

Jordan would never remember how long they trudged through the blinding snow, battling the wind and the icy pellets that beat against their unprotected faces. This wasn't a gentle snowfall. It was a full-fledged blizzard, carrying as much icy sleet as snow in its frigid winds.

She was exhausted. Each breath became more labored and ragged. Her lungs were burning from the abuse. Her legs throbbed painfully and her muscles were cramped from the cold.

When she was sure she was about to drop, Reeves reached for her hand and virtually dragged her along behind him. She was about to object to their rigorous pace when she realized that he had altered their direction. They were now moving laterally. She raised her head and peered out from beneath the blanket. A dark shadow against the gray-white world took form. It was a shed.

She hastened her leaden footsteps. In a matter of moments they collapsed together against the weathered exterior wall of the small building. They gasped for air, waiting long minutes until their heartbeats had slowed considerably and their respiration was closer to normal.

Without moving his body as he leaned against the wall, Reeves turned his head and looked at her. "How are you doing?" He smiled, and that in itself warmed Jordan.

She rested her head on his shoulder and murmured, "I'm fine."

"Let's see if we can get into this . . . whatever it is."

"It's a tool shed. They dot the sides of the mountains." She explained. "If a farmer has a pasture in the higher elevations, he uses these tool sheds to store equipment and supplies. That way he doesn't have to haul it up and down the mountain."

"Very ingenious. I could kiss our farmer."

She laughed in spite of their grim circumstances.

Reeves tried the door and found that it hadn't even been locked. "Trusting soul," he commented as he went in first to check out the shelter. He swung wide the door and said, "Hey, this is great. Jordan come on in."

She stepped through the low door and her eyes scanned the single room. Its walls were as rough as the exterior, but they were sturdy and snug. There were several hand tools stashed in one corner, a dismantled plow in another. A wooden bucket was hanging by a peg on one wall. On the wall opposite the door stood an ancient Franklin stove.

"I think they were expecting us," Reeves laughed as he crossed the room, rubbing his hands together. He knelt down to inspect the stove. "There's even some wood here," he said excitedly.

Jordan laughed, happy to be safe inside the shelter and not still roaming aimlessly through the storm. She took the blanket off her head and shook her hair free. She spread the blanket over the tools, hoping it would dry out. The wet smell of wool mingled with the close, musty smell of the tool shed, but to her, at that moment, the enclosure seemed like paradise.

Reeves stood up and brushed his hands clean of the soot he had picked up from the stove. For long moments they stood there, staring at each other over the expanse of rough plank flooring. They had come through a harrowing experience and survived it. And as tragedy does to those who have shared it—even to strangers—it cemented their relationship.

She took one shaky step toward him and then he was there, clasping her in his arms as if he'd never let her go. He buried his face in her hair, murmuring incoherent words that were clear enough to her, for it was the emotion they conveyed that was important. Her arms wrapped around his waist and she pressed herself as close to him as she could. Tears streamed down her cheeks and she blotted them with the soft knit of his sweater.

"What is this?" he asked gently as he tilted her head up. "Tears? Don't you like the idea of being marooned with me? Hm?" He smiled tenderly.

"I was scared, Reeves."

"Didn't I tell you I'd take care of you? Don't you trust me?"

"Yes, but I—"

"It's all right," he comforted as he smoothed her hair

141

back from her pale, troubled face. "I was scared too for a while. But I was confident that something would turn up and it did. Now I've repaid you for saving me during the thunderstorm."

She nestled close to him again, savoring his strength, which flowed into her, warming her. "You were no trouble." Then a mischievous sparkle came into her blue-ringed gray eyes as she looked up at him. "I'd have done the same for anyone."

He pushed her away from him, though he kept his hands tight on her arms. "Do you want me to kick your little fanny out in the snow again?" he asked, scowling at her menacingly.

"Would you?" she asked, swaying toward him slightly and reaching for him provocatively.

He broke into another wide grin and crushed her against him. "Hell, no. You know I wouldn't." Demanding lips came down on hers like a scorching brand. His hands were bold as they moved over her body, touching her, claiming her. Jordan was breathless, but his mouth was ruthless and didn't settle for less than total abdication. When at last he pulled away, she sagged against him.

"I surrender," she sighed.

He chuckled. "Now we're even. Just remember that if we're ever shipwrecked on a desert island, it's your turn again to rescue me." He kissed her quickly. "Now we'd better scout around here and see what we can see. You bring in the things from outside and I'll try to start a fire in this stove. I hope nothing has clogged the chimney," he mused aloud as he inspected the joints of the metal chimney.

She brought in her backpack, the picnic basket, and his

camera from where they had left them under the narrow overhang of the roof. While he crouched in front of the stove, arranging the wood and striking the matches someone had obligingly left on a shelf, she cautiously explored among the tools. Behind them she found two tarps that were moldy and dusty, but would help insulate the floor. She spread them out near the stove, where Reeves had been successful in starting a fire.

"We have enough wood for a while, if we don't splurge on it. I'll see if some is stored outside. If my guess is right, this shed has served this purpose before. That bucket looks like the kind one would use to haul water. I'll bet there's a stream close by. I'm going to try to find it."

"No," Jordan cried in a high, tense voice. "Reeves, please don't go out again."

"I'll be all right. I'll keep the shed in sight. I need to try to find us some water before dark."

"What time is it?" she asked. It was already gloomy outside.

"After seven o'clock. How did I manage to sleep so long out there?" he asked.

"You were relaxed."

His brows hooded his eyes as he looked at her devilishly. "Well, some parts of me were relaxed, while other parts—"

"Reeves!" she rebuked him softly.

He was laughing as he took the bucket from the peg on the wall. "I'll be right back. You stay inside no matter how long I'm gone."

"Be careful."

He cradled her cheek with his free hand. "I promise.

143

Kiss me good-bye." She went up on her toes and kissed him sweetly on the mouth.

He didn't speak again before he went out into the storm and slammed the door behind him. Left alone, Jordan paced the shed restlessly, listening for the sound of his return. She went to the stove, picked up a log from the stack, remembered that they must be conservative, and returned it.

She checked the blanket. It was still damp, so she moved it nearer the fire. She was nervous and her nerves only increased a problem that had been plaguing her for an hour or more. Why had she drunk so much wine with lunch?

"I won't think about it," she said aloud. But the harder she tried not to think about it, the more aware of her discomfort she became. Finally, she decided there was only one solution. She would have to go outside and relieve the problem.

At the door, she listened to the howling wind and almost changed her mind, but she flung open the door before she could think about it any longer. She pulled the door firmly closed behind her. Huddling against the wind, she scuttled around one side of the building. The land sloped away from it and the immediate area had been cleared of trees. She decided it was too wide open. Dashing around to the back of the shed, she saw a crib where firewood and heavier farm implements had been stored. She stepped over the rail of the crib and hid herself between the stacks of wood.

When she was done, she refastened her jeans, sighing in tremendous relief. She wasted no time in climbing out of the crib and running back to the front of the shed.

With her head lowered in protection from the stinging wind, she didn't see Reeves before she ran headlong into him. She jerked her head up. His eyes were wild, his mouth anguished. He held her in a death grip. Stumbling over their own feet, he dragged her back into the shed and shut the door, still clasping her to him.

"God, Jordan, don't ever do that to me again." His voice was quivering. "You scared the hell out of me." He dropped to the tarps on the floor and took several heaving breaths.

She wasn't sure what she had done, but she stammered an apology, "I'm . . . I'm sorry . . . I didn't . . ."

"I came back in and you weren't here. I thought you had gone out to find me. I died a thousand deaths." He reached up and grabbed her hand, pulled her down beside him, and held her close. "Where were you?"

"I had to go to the bathroom."

He laughed then in relief. "I didn't think of that."

She leaned against him. "Did you get some water?"

"Yeah." He indicated the full bucket standing next to the stove. "But in light of what you just did to me, you can't drink any."

"Tyrant."

"That's right. I'm a jealous despot." He kissed her with hard, unyielding lips. "This is my castle and don't you forget it."

"You'd better treat me nice. I know where the extra firewood is hidden," she said cockily.

He tweaked her nose. "So do I. I saw it on my way out."

"Oh." She gnawed her bottom lip in make-believe helplessness. "Then pray tell, Exalted One, what I can do to stay in your good graces." Her eyelashes fluttered so comically that Reeves bit his lip to keep from bursting out with laughter.

He stretched out on the tarp and propped himself on his elbows. "I don't know. I'll be thinking on it while you serve me dinner."

"Yes, Your Majesty." She bowed her head and then, when she raised it, stuck out her tongue at him.

"Thirty lashes," he roared, pointing a condemning finger at her.

She faked a swoon that brought her along his side in a most delicious proximity. "Oh, kind sir, I beg you to have mercy." She shifted her weight until she was leaning over him.

"Very well. Thirty lashes or thirty kisses."

She considered her alternatives for a moment, her eyes squinted and her brow furrowed. "Thirty lashes," she said impudently. Immediately she was rolled to her back and pinned beneath him.

"I've changed my mind. No mercy," he growled before he kissed her. What had started out playfully soon became serious, and her arms folded across his neck. A sea of passion engulfed them and it was long moments before they broke the surface.

He dropped light kisses on each feature of her face. "Jordan?"

"Hm?"

"I'm starving."

"How romantic."

"I've got to keep up my strength," he said defensively.

"So you can blaze a trail down the mountain?"

His eyes lit up with a wicked gleam. "Oh, what I could do with that leading line," he said. "But you'd probably slap my face, so I'll just say that blazing a trail down the mountain is only one course I plan to chart."

She blushed to the roots of her hair and hastily jumped to her feet. "I'll get the food ready. At least we'll eat well as long as we're stranded."

The blanket was drying, but Jordan decided to leave it where it was. They could spread out their supper on the tarp. Reeves pulled his sweater over his head. He had taken off the windbreaker when he came in from the stream. "If you'll excuse my bad manners, I'm going to take this thing off. Hauling the water was exerting. Not to mention . . . other stimulation."

She tried to keep her eyes away from his chest, but couldn't. She watched as he poured water from the bucket over a handkerchief and bathed his face, neck, and chest with the damp cloth. It reminded her of the time he had dried himself with her towel after she had let him in out of the rain.

Had that only been four days ago? Four days. Yet they were so familiar. She recognized his facial expressions and was able to interpret them. His tones of voice, his gestures were as familiar to her as her own—probably more so. Some lovers, she felt sure, didn't know each other near this well even after being together for years.

She and Reeves wouldn't have years. Days? Hours? The thought shattered her. She loved him, but he would walk out of her life as unexpectedly as he had walked into it. When the next disaster struck, he and his camera would be on their way to witness it. And she would be left behind with nothing but bittersweet memories.

Her face must have revealed some of her thoughts, for when he turned around Reeves looked at her closely. "Jordan? Is something wrong?"

Embarrassed at being caught, she stuttered, "Nnnno. I . . . I . . . You're all cleaned up and I must look terrible." She scrambled across the tarp and picked up her backpack, putting her back to him. "Can you give me a minute?"

"Take your time. I'll pour the wine."

"You'll let me drink wine again?" she asked over her shoulder as she peeled off her sweater.

"Only in moderation," he said with mock seriousness.

Jordan took a mirror out of her backpack, thankful that she had brought along a few grooming items. Her cheeks didn't need artificial color. They were rosy from the wind and cold. To prevent chapping, she smoothed a moisturizing lotion on them. Her eyes were sparkling in the firelight so she didn't bother to add more eye makeup. She whisked on a dollop of lip gloss and brushed her hair vigorously.

Luckily she had brought a purse atomizer of Norell, and she misted it around her neck and chest. Eyeing herself critically, she thought she didn't look bad for being stranded on a mountain. Hesitantly, she unbuttoned the first three buttons of the oxford cloth blouse to relieve its severity.

When she turned around, Reeves whistled long and low. She laughed. "Thank you. I know I don't deserve such a lavish compliment, but I appreciate it anyway."

"You look terrific," he said warmly, and his eyes told her he was sincere.

They ate slowly, and when their hunger was abated, Reeves said, "We can put the basket near the door to preserve the meats and cheeses."

"How long do you think the storm will last?" Jordan asked.

He shrugged. "I don't know. Since it's the first of the season, it probably won't be too bad. We'll reassess the situation in the morning."

Tacitly they agreed not to discuss their departure from this tool shed that had conveniently provided them with a time and place of their own, away from the rest of the world. They would only face going back when they must. For now they would be grateful to the storm for making this encapsulation necessary.

Neither of them mentioned Helmut, though both knew that he must be frantic with worry about them. What would he think of them spending the night together? It didn't matter. Nothing mattered except their solitude in this mountain retreat.

"Look! Another box of chocolates!" Jordan exclaimed happily, and took the discovered treasure out of the hamper. Reeves snatched the box from her hands.

"Let me have some this time. You ate every one of them at lunch."

"You had two pieces," she argued.

"You were keeping count?" he teased, and held the box out of her reach.

As it ended up, they shared them equally. She fed Reeves his ration bite by bite and, when her fingertips became sticky and chocolate covered, he licked them clean.

She watched as he gently sucked each fingertip. His tongue laved it. A tight, tickling sensation welled up in her throat to match the one in the center of her body. Involuntarily her eyes closed. "I never knew that eating chocolates could be such an erotic experience," she whispered.

"I never knew a woman could be so sexy without even trying."

They kissed. They kissed again.

"We'd better gather up the food," she mumbled against his lips.

He grumbled an "All right," and began to help her.

When everything was replaced in the basket and it was set next to the door, she returned to the tarp with the thermos of coffee and the bottle of cognac.

"I don't know if this is still hot, but we'll see." She uncapped the thermos and the smell of fresh hot coffee wafted out. "It is!"

She poured each of them a cup of the steaming coffee and added a capful of cognac while Reeves spread the now dry blanket over the tarps. They took off their boots and socks and stretched their bare feet out close to the stove, whose chimney was drawing well despite its ramshackle appearance.

Jordan sipped her coffee slowly, the cognac burning in her stomach. "I think I'm getting drunk," she said softly as she leaned against Reeves. She was settled between his thighs, her back to his chest.

"Good. I plan to take advantage of you."

She slapped him on the knee and he yelped. "What?" she asked in alarm. Then she noticed the raw, red skin on his knees. "Oh, Reeves. I hope you don't get frostbite."

"No, they're just chapped."

"Here, I've got something for them." She crawled across the blanket toward her backpack and came back with the plastic bottle of lotion she had used on her cheeks.

"Does it burn?" he asked suspiciously.

"Like fire."

"No thank you," he said, and moved his legs away from her.

She laughed as she reached out a hand to capture one of his legs. "You big chicken. I was only teasing. It'll make them feel better."

With soothing strokes she applied the lotion to the reddened skin. She smothered a giggle, then another. "What's so funny?" he asked huffily.

"I've never put lotion on hairy legs before." He tried to look offended, but couldn't, and they both laughed. The lotion was put aside when she was finished and they resumed their former position. They stared into the flames.

"This is when I really miss a cigarette," Reeves said after a spell of companionable silence. "It's not just the tobacco I miss. It's the relaxing activity." He sighed theatrically. "I guess I'll have to find another relaxing activity for my hands."

Before the sentence was completed, he matched action to words. His hand slipped under her arm and curved around her until his hand covered her breast. He flexed his fingers, not quite squeezing her.

She snuggled closer to him. "Speaking of your hands, this is the one you cut, isn't it?" She removed his hand from her breast and saw the telltale red marks across three of his fingers. Each one was kissed in turn.

"Jordan, do me a favor," he murmured into her hair.

"Is it illegal or illicit?"

"We'll get to those favors later. This is a simple request."

"What?"

151

"Would you take this off?" He took her left hand and touched the large diamond ring on the third finger.

Words weren't necessary. She knew how he must resent that symbol of her relationship with Helmut. The ring was slipped off her finger and zippered into a small compartment of her backpack.

Silently she came back into his arms. He eased her around to face him. Gently he cupped her head in his large, capable hands and drew her upward until her lips met his. The kiss conveyed a tenderness that conversely broke down all barriers she might have constructed in her mind. Whatever the future held for them, tonight belonged to her and Reeves. One night out of a lifetime wasn't asking too much. Whatever the cost, she wasn't going to deny this to herself.

The consequences could be met later, the piper paid later, but not now. Not now, when his mouth invaded the hollows of hers. Not when his hands touched her so exquisitely that her mind reeled under the impact.

"Jordan," he groaned softly, and pushed her away slightly. "I want to see all of you." His fingers deliberately and deftly worked the buttons of her blouse until it hung free. With self-imposed, agonizing care, he eased it over her shoulders.

His eyes dropped to her chest. The sheer lacy bra was a voyeur's dream. It hid nothing, enhanced everything. The glossy flesh-toned fabric made her skin beneath it glisten. The rosy nipples pressed against that tight, shimmering veil invitingly, daring the observer to touch and kiss.

Self-denial became Reeves's obsession. His thumbs hooked under the satin straps and gradually pulled them from her shoulders and upper arms, staring all the while at the two perfectly shaped breasts that were revealed to him by tiny degrees.

Finally his patience was rewarded and they fell free of the gossamer fetter. Only then did he unclasp the garment and remove it completely.

Jordan had remained motionless, watching his face and the tender expressions so apparent on it. It gave her a heady, victorious feeling to know that she could evoke such emotion from him. Had he asked her to, she would have torn the bra from her body. But she knew, as did he, that this way was better.

Just as a connoisseur glories in the properties of the wine, studies its color, its bouquet, twirls it in his glass, before taking the first sip, so had Reeves treasured her before availing himself of her body.

His eyes wandered over her, taking in the creamy texture of her skin, the delicate color of the crests, the gentle curves that flagrantly declared her femininity. Then his hands joined his eyes in that most pleasant expedition.

"You're beautifully made," he said gruffly. The dark russet hair tickled her skin as he dipped his head and kissed her breasts, each in turn, lingeringly, slowly.

They had all night.

In silent agreement they backed away from each other. He rid himself of the rest of his clothes. She shyly stepped out of her jeans, but left on the wispy protection of sheer panties.

When they were lying on one half of the blanket, covered by the other half, he pulled her to him. His heavy leg rested on hers, moving hypnotically.

She caught the sides of his head in eager hands and drew him down to her lips. His tongue plunged deep into her mouth. She grew dizzy under its avid searching and clasped his shoulders to keep from falling into the sublime abyss that lured her so seductively.

"I've got to have you, Jordan." His words were barely audible as his mouth left hers to plant kisses across her chest. Her breasts were gently ravaged. Twin buds of desire rose up to meet the wet heat of his mouth. He gave as much as he took. His tongue and lips blessed her with the honey of his mouth.

"Don't stop," she begged when he moved his lips away from her tingling breasts. But the request went unheeded as his mouth trailed over her stomach and past her navel. "Reeves . . . !" she gasped when she felt that urgent sweetness tugging on her skin in places that had never known a kiss before.

Her panties were dragged down her hips and legs until she was free of them. Still kissing her, his hand slipped between the slender columns of her thighs and touched her where she most longed to know him.

His fingers commenced a gentle exploration that began as a mere fluttering but became a stroking search that knew no bounds.

"Sweet . . . you feel . . . Look at me, Jordan, please . . . look at me while I touch you. . . . Precious . . ."

She obeyed every command and heedlessly raced toward the culmination his hands and mouth promised.

"Say you want me," he pleaded. His fingers bespoke an entreaty all their own.

"I do," she moaned.

"Say it, Jordan. Tell me."

He covered her with his own body and she felt the hard, throbbing evidence of his desire against the insides of her thighs. "I want you, Reeves." She shuddered at his tentative probing. "Please."

Then he was inside her, strong and massive, filling her completely, eliminating a void, giving her all of himself.

He buried his face in the fragrant cloud of her black hair and whispered endearments, accolades. Her hands locked behind his back.

His head, lying next to hers, turned until he was looking at her and he said, "Don't move for a while. Just surround me. . . . You can't know how good it feels."

"Explain it to me."

And he did, in a language that their bodies understood long before their minds could grasp its import.

9

‹••••••••••••»

What do you want to be when you grow up?"

She laughed and snuggled closer to him, if that were possible, and settled her lips at the base of his throat. "Don't you think I'm grown up already?" she purred as she nibbled at his neck.

"You're grown up in all the right places." His hands admired those places.

Temporarily their passion had been slaked. They were cuddled together under the single blanket. The floor was hard underneath them, but neither noticed. Jordan's backpack, emptied of its contents and wrapped in

Reeves's sweater, served as their pillow. The logs in the stove, well seasoned, crackled and hissed cheerfully. The golden reflection of the flames danced on the dark walls.

His fingers traced her spine. "Do you intend to stay in that newsstand for the rest of your life?"

"I can't. I was fired."

The fingers stilled. "Fired? When? Why?"

She laughed softly. "Yes, to the first question. This morning to the second. Because my boss saw the story about my engagement to Helmut and assumed that I wouldn't be needing my job anymore to the third. The boss's daughter inherited my position before my corpse was cold," she said lightly.

"Sonofa—That was a rotten thing to have happen. No wonder you were so mad at me this morning. I'm sorry, Jordan. Can I help? Is there something I can do?"

"No. At first I was upset, to say the least. Now"—she moved one slender leg between the warmth of his— "now it doesn't seem to matter so much. The job in Lucerne has served its purpose. After Charles's death, I needed to live and work, breathe, without the interference of well-intentioned friends and my parents. This time I've spent in Switzerland has been like a three-year vacation. I need to find something to do that's more challenging and productive."

"Will you return to the States?" Studiously they were avoiding talking of Helmut and the role he would play in her future. He was there, lurking in the background of their minds, but neither wanted to speak his name aloud. Apparently, since he was asking about her going back to America, Reeves had finally accepted her insistence that she wasn't going to marry the Swiss.

"Yes, probably, but I don't know where," she replied. "I think I'll try to find a nice, quiet place and settle down to write. That's something I've always aspired to do."

"What type of material do you want to write?"

"Sex manuals," she quipped.

"How-tos?"

"Yes."

A laugh vibrated his chest, where she rested her head. "Oh, yeah?" He clasped her to him and rolled her atop him. "That requires a lot of research, you know."

"I'm willing to sacrifice whatever is necessary," she teased, and leaned down to taste his mouth. It tasted like her own. "Are you willing to be a guinea pig?"

"Oink."

She collapsed with laughter. "Guinea pigs don't oink, you dope."

"No? What do they do?"

She showed him, and the subject of her immediate future was forgotten.

"So after your first sex manual is a bestseller, then what?"

With the blanket wrapped around them, they were sitting facing the fire. "I'll never write a sex manual." She jabbed him in the ribs.

"It's the world's loss. You're an expert." He kissed the end of her nose. "What are you going to write?"

"Travel tips for an American in Europe? Fiction? I haven't decided yet. My priority is settling down and carving out my niche in the universe. What about you?"

"I guess I'll keep on globe-trotting with my trusty camera."

"Oh."

It would seem that their goals in life were as opposite as east is from west. Again the subject of their future was left alone. He pulled her onto his lap. They had no future beyond the walls of the tool shed.

"I'm starved," he whispered against her ear. They were lying entwined under the blanket. Her legs fit snugly between his. It would be hard to determine which limb belonged to whom. Their arms were wrapped around each other.

"You've got an insatiable appetite."

"I know. And I'm always hungry, too."

She raised her head and looked down into mischievous green eyes. "Are we talking about the same kind of appetite?"

"Ohhhhh, you're talking about *food.*"

She swatted him on the bottom and disentangled her arms and legs. "What would you like for breakfast? Smoked oysters or pâté?"

"Ugh!"

"How about bread and butter?"

"That's better."

She took a loaf of bread and the butter out of the picnic hamper beside the door and brought it back to him. He watched lazily as she liberally spread butter on the bread and handed it to him.

"You aren't hungry?" he asked when she didn't fix anything for herself.

"No. Just remember, if we're stuck in here for days, that you owe me one ration of bread and butter."

While he munched, Jordan toyed with his ears. She rubbed the lobes between her fingers. Then her hands moved down his neck and shoulders, massaging as they went.

"You do that very well," he remarked, then took another huge bite of bread.

Jordan was somewhat piqued that he could accept her evocative ministrations so blithely. Determinedly she allowed her fingertips to lightly brush across his chest. His enthusiastic chewing ceased abruptly. Her smooth oval fingertips found the flat, brown nipples unerringly. He swallowed hard.

"I don't suppose you'd want to occupy yourself with some other pastime while I finish my breakfast, would you?" he asked in a low, throaty voice.

Her lips curved upward in a gamine smile as she shook her head no and moved closer to him. Her hair trailed across his face bewitchingly. She lowered her head and tormented with her flicking tongue what her fingers had brought to hard distension.

"Jordan—" he gasped. "God, that feels good. How . . . how did you know to do this?"

"Instinct," she breathed against his skin.

"God bless Mother Nature."

He couldn't say more. Her mouth continued to amuse itself on his chest while her hands slid lower down his torso.

His breath was trapped in his lungs, longing to burst free. He waited in anguished anticipation until her fingers combed through the dark thatch on his abdomen and beyond. Only then did a soft, almost painful moan escape from his throat. He fell back against the blanket.

Frugal as they must be with their food, the crust of bread was tossed, forgotten, into a corner.

"Is this—"

"Heaven?" he interrupted. "Yes, it's heaven."

"Do you like—"

"Do you have to ask?"

"I want you to tell me."

He opened his eyes and searched her anxious expression. She was still almost virginal, innocent, nervous, wanting to please him. His face softened as he placed his palms on both sides of her face. "Yes, yes. Touch me, Jordan."

Her mouth was brutalized by lips that conquered with finesse. Her breasts were attacked by hands whose strength lay in the persuasion of their tender touch. Her nipples were lashed by a rough-soft tongue that was only a harbinger to greedy lips tempered by gentleness.

By now their bodies were so well acquainted that he knew the instant she was ready to receive him. He plunged into her, deeper, fuller, more certain of his right to be there than ever before. Every part of him, the man he was, the man he aspired to be, concentrated in that mysterious haven that belonged uniquely to Jordan. He felt enriched, emboldened, empowered, and for the first time in his life knew the spiritual heights of loving as well as the physical.

"I meant what I said that first night," he said hoarsely in her ear.

"What?" It wasn't a word. It was a soft expulsion of breath that only he could understand.

"It's never been like this for me, Jordan." On the last word, the tumult came and he repeated her name in a rhythmic meter. That's why he couldn't hear the soft words she chanted into his shoulder. "I love you I love you I love you."

* * *

"Jordan? Are you awake?"

"Yes."

"It's getting light outside."

"Is it?"

"Yes." He stirred slightly and arched his head backward. "I can see daylight through the crack under the door." The woman beside him didn't move and he resumed his original position with his chin resting on the crown of her head. "The wind isn't blowing."

She sighed heavily but only hugged him tighter. "Do you think the storm is over?" The words were more portentous than either of them wanted to admit.

"Yes." He didn't feel inclined to move either. Halfheartedly he said, "We really should get up and dress."

"Yes, I suppose you're right."

"I don't want to," he groaned.

"I don't either."

They clung to each other tenaciously and kissed with desperate passion. They knew their idyll was over. Someone would come looking for them.

Helmut.

They got up and dressed silently, suddenly shy of each other. After hours of immodest, total nakedness, they now averted their heads. Their conversation, when they dared to speak at all, was trite, and so they dropped the embarrassing effort. Everything that could be said had been.

Reeves opened the door and looked out. The mountainside was blanketed with snow, but it wasn't very deep. The sky was still cloudy, but not oppressive. The wind had diminished to a breeze that barely disturbed the clumps of snow in the pine needles on the trees.

"I think we can make it down once we get a bearing on where we are. We'll take it slow."

"All right," she answered listlessly. While Reeves banked the fire so it would harmlessly burn itself out, she folded the tarps and stored them where they had been.

Reeves pulled on his windbreaker and zipped it closed. He insisted that she wrap the blanket around her, though they didn't think the cold air would be nearly so bad without the howling wind of last evening. When the backpack, the camera case, and the picnic basket were divided as they had been the day before, they left the sanctuary of the shed.

Jordan took one slow, sweeping glance around the small room, ostensibly to make sure they hadn't over-looked anything. Actually she wanted to fix it firmly in her mind, to safeguard it forever in her memory. Tears made the snow-covered landscape look watery as she followed Reeves out of the shed. She trekked along behind his lead.

Cautiously, but easily, they reached the edge of the timberline. Soon after they cleared it, they saw the search party below them snaking up the side of the mountain. There must have been thirty or forty men in mountain climbing attire fanned out in a long horizontal line on the hillside.

Reeves stopped and surveyed the sight with a wry grin on his face. "You can tell by the thoroughness of the operation that Helmut's in charge."

Jordan didn't respond. Instead she shifted his camera case from one arm to the other and followed him as he started down again. What would she tell Helmut? Would he ask about last night? Would he know without asking?

Surely if she and Reeves looked at each other the truth about their night together would reveal itself.

But the closer they came to the group of men looking for them, the tighter the lines around Reeves's mouth became. His eyes weren't shining with a glow of passion as they had done all night. Instead they seemed to reflect the icy patches of snow he skirted around on their careful descent. They were cold.

Anxiety seared her chest, and it was far more painful than her hard breathing. In some secret part of her heart she had hoped that they might reconcile their ambitions for the future, compromise on what they wanted out of life. The splendor of last night couldn't be so easily dismissed, could it?

"They've seen us," said Reeves, tersely breaking into her thoughts. He set down the heavy basket and waved both arms high over his head.

Jordan saw one of the men respond by enthusiastically waving back. He was wearing a bright red ski jacket and tight black pants tucked into cleated boots. He was unmistakably Helmut. She watched as he turned to excuse most of the men with him, correctly guessing that she and Reeves were safe if they were walking down. Ten or twelve of the men remained with him as he continued to climb.

"Let's wait for them," Reeves suggested, and gratefully set down his load. Jordan did likewise. She folded the blanket into a thick cushion, placed it on a wide, flat rock, and they sat down on it. By the time the snow soaked through it, Helmut would be there.

The silence that strained between them grew more tense with each moment. Finally Reeves stirred and let his eyes skim her face before flickering away.

"Jordan, about last night . . ." He sighed.

Here it comes, she thought. The gradual letdown. Don't cause a scene. Be calm. Don't weep or tear at your hair.

"I . . . I never planned for it to happen with us again. After that night of the storm, when I learned you were engaged, I swore I'd leave you alone. But then you said that you weren't going to marry Helmut . . . that day on the mountain and then yesterday morning . . . being stranded and all—"

"Don't talk about last night, Reeves. Please." By an act of will, she prevented the tears that flooded her eyes from overflowing.

Almost on a whisper he asked, "Then you know how I feel about it?"

Yes, she knew. For her it had been a turning point in her life. Had she ever doubted that she was making the right decision not to marry Helmut, she saw clearly now that such a marriage would never come about. Foolish though it was to love a man who had no commitments beyond the next fast-breaking news story, she loved Reeves. Marriage to another man would be unthinkable.

For Reeves it had been an episode. She had been a brief but pleasant interlude in his life. He had found her to be genial, attractive, and—she swallowed—obliging. He had responded as any man would, given the same set of circumstances. Reading anything other than fierce passion into their lovemaking was childish and futile and wrong.

She gulped down a sob. "Yes, I know what it meant to you, Reeves," she answered with far more serenity in her voice than she had a right to expect.

"Good," he said with obvious relief.

They saw Helmut striding toward them now. The look on his face, even through his fatigue, was one of elation.

"Jordan, since you understand about last night, I want you to know I'm leaving immediately. I'm going to Paris tonight."

The words pierced her as no others had. So soon! He was ridding himself of her quickly. The severance would be swift, clean, and irrevocable.

She didn't look at him or respond. She wouldn't let him see the tears. He'd never know the heartache she was suffering. The death her spirit was dying would be a private one, witnessed by no one. He must never know that she loved him.

Not hesitating until it was too late, she catapulted off their resting place and ran pell mell down the hill, scrambling over the slippery surface. "Helmut!" she shouted. Let Reeves think their time together had been only a casual dalliance for her, too. Let him think she was going back to her wealthy fiancé. Let him think the worst of Jordan Hadlock, but don't let him see that she loved him.

Helmut was waiting for her with outstretched arms, and, when she threw herself into them, he thought the tears that bathed her face were tears of joy.

"My darling, my darling," he said comfortingly as he patted her back. "Everything's all right. You're safe now. Was it too ghastly?"

Ghastly? Hysteria came very close to the surface. Paradise? Shangri-la? Utopia? Yes. But never ghastly. "I . . . I'm just glad to see you," she said as she continued to cling to him. By shutting her eyes she could blot out everything else.

Helmut instructed one of the men to give her something warm to drink. The fellow must have obeyed because Helmut was soon pressing a silver cup against her lips. "Here, darling, drink a sip. It will start to warm you."

The hot coffee was generously laced with brandy and she choked on the first swallow. His hand was running briskly up and down her back. "Slowly, my dear, slowly. We won't start back down until you're ready. No storm is forecast for tonight. I blame myself for not checking the weather report before we started out yesterday. That first storm was expected in the higher elevations. I could have prevented this entire nightmare."

How glad she was that she and Reeves had been innocent of the storm predictions. They couldn't be held accountable. They had been victims.

"Reeves, you seem hale and hearty enough despite your ordeal," Helmut beamed. She didn't turn around, though she heard Reeves's footsteps crunching on the snow. "Someone pour this man a drink," Helmut ordered. "I'm eager to hear how you managed to survive the night and come out of it seemingly unscathed and none the worse for wear."

Jordan rotated slowly in Helmut's arms and saw Reeves take a cup similar to the one she was drinking from. He sipped the hot coffee and thanked both Helmut and his assistant.

"After eating that bountiful lunch you brought along, Jordan and I decided to walk it off and go farther up the mountain. We sat down to rest awhile and . . ." His voice trailed off. Green eyes slid to Jordan, where she was still leaning against Helmut. The eyes bore into her and

Reeves's voice was hard when he continued. "We fell asleep. When we woke up, it was snowing."

Briefly he outlined their halting trip back down the mountain until they discovered the tool shed. "Luckily we were able to take refuge there."

Again his eyes flew to Jordan and again she read the open hostility and scorn there. He ignored her then as he turned back to Helmut. "Before the night was over, we were grateful both to a benevolent farmer and to your picnic basket."

Helmut laughed then and clapped Reeves on the shoulder. "Thank you for taking care of my girl for me."

Jordan winced at the words. She dared to look up at Reeves. A disdainful sneer marred the handsome features of his face. "She's a woman easily pleased." The underlying insult was understood only by her, but she caught his disparagement and resented it highly. She hadn't exactly ripped off his clothes and chased him around that shed until he finally submitted to her!

She turned back to Helmut and asked, "What about your airplane?"

He stroked her cheek with a loving finger. "How like you, Jordan, darling, to be worried about someone else's crisis when living through one of your own. My pilot crash landed the aircraft. He, the crew, and the cargo were all intact."

"I'm so glad," she said.

He raised her hand to kiss it and exclaimed, "Jordan, where is your ring? Not lost in the storm I hope."

"No, it . . . I . . ." She looked helplessly toward Reeves but his face gave away nothing of what he was thinking. It could have been carved out of stone. The green eyes glinted frigidly. "It's in my backpack," she muttered at last.

"Fetch me that." Helmut pointed to the backpack one of his men had retrieved. Once he had it in his hands, it was only a matter of moments before he found the diamond ring zippered into one of the many pockets.

He slid the cold metal ring onto Jordan's nerveless finger and said with deep satisfaction, "There. Things are back to where they should be."

But nothing was as it should be. She raised mournful eyes to Reeves, but the spot where he had been standing was empty. As Helmut pulled her into an encompassing embrace, over his shoulder she saw that Reeves was already stalking away from them on his way down the mountain.

Knowing that this might well be the last time she would ever see him, she whispered, "My love, my life. I'll love you forever."

Hearing her words and mistakenly interpreting them, Helmut hugged her tighter.

10

~~~~~~~~~~~~~~~~~~~~~~~

"Thank you for coming by, Helmut," Jordan said as she shut the door of the bookstore behind him, put the closed sign in the window, and pulled down the shade.

"Darling, I was in the middle of a very important meeting." His irritation at her summoning him and insisting that she see him immediately was apparent. "I confess to a certain confusion. I fail to see the urgency you intimated."

"I apologize, Helmut. But I didn't want to postpone this meeting any longer." She led him up the stairs to her apartment and switched on the lamps in the living room. She offered him a chair and sat down on the sofa.

"Helmut, I'm not going to marry you."

There. She had said it. It hadn't been so difficult. There was no resultant pain. Why had she not said it before? He wasn't threatening her with reprisals. He wasn't shouting deprecations. In fact, he wasn't doing anything but staring at her blankly, as if she had suddenly lost her faculties.

When he recovered from the shocking statement, he leaned forward in his chair and searched her face for signs of mental imbalance. "My dear, you're unwell. Surely you can't mean what you just said. You're not thinking clearly. Maybe—"

"I'm quite well, Helmut. Actually, I feel better than I have in a long time. I meant what I said. I'm not going to marry you."

His managerial training took over and he relaxed once more against the back of his chair. He crossed one ankle over the opposite knee. "I've noticed a change in you since the night you were trapped on the mountain in the storm. It was a stressful experience. Perhaps you were traumatized by it. These things happen, you know. I think, given time, you'll be restored to your normally healthy outlook and will start thinking rationally again."

He was so self-confident that Jordan smiled fondly. She shook her head. "No, Helmut. I had decided not to marry you long before then. Time won't change my mind."

He was quiet for long moments, weighing the firm conviction in her voice, watching her unwavering expression. "But why, darling?" he asked at last.

"Helmut, I have a deep affection for you. We've shared some happy times. I'll never be able to thank you for your unlimited generosity, nor will I ever forget your

171

many kindnesses." She got up and walked around the end of the couch. Her fingers examined the piping around the cushions as she said, "But I don't love you in the way a wife should love a husband. A marriage without love would be unfair to both of us. We are miles apart in our backgrounds, literally and figuratively. I would never fit into your world."

"Let me be the judge of that, Jordan," he said.

She smiled. "I don't doubt your acumen for making executive decisions, Helmut, but this is a decision of the heart. Of emotions. I'm not an employee that you can groom for a certain position in your conglomerate."

"Is that the impression I give you? I'm sorry. I never intended to make you feel as though I were molding you into something you weren't."

"Which brings me to the next point," she said. "Perhaps right now you *do* find me diverting. I'm not like the many other women you've paid court to. But how long would the novelty last? When would you grow tired of me?"

"I love you the way you are, Jordan."

"For life?" Her question hit home. He looked away quickly and she knew that her words had caused him to think of her as he never had before. "I had one disastrous marriage. That was enough. I wouldn't want to ever make you unhappy."

"You wouldn't," he said adamantly.

"I would, Helmut. I want tranquillity. My former husband promised me a home and children, stability, security. He never delivered. And while your means and abilities far surpass his, I would soon tire of your hectic pace. I'm an old-fashioned American girl with Midwest ideas ingrained into me. I've loved every minute I've lived abroad, Helmut, and I wouldn't trade the experience, but I want to go home. Please forgive me if this disappoints you. It's for the best. I promise you."

"Why did you ever accept my proposal if you felt it weren't for the best?" he asked with just a trace of aristocratic hauteur.

"Did I ever accept? Officially?" she teased.

For the first time, he smiled. It was a rueful grin. "I guess you didn't. I'm accustomed to getting my way." With customary conceit he added, "It never occurred to me that you might not want to marry me."

She laughed. "Helmut, you're priceless." She took the velvet ring box out of her skirt pocket and went to the place where he was now standing beside the chair. "Here is your ring."

"I don't suppose you'd consider keeping it as a token of my esteem." Jordan smiled, but shook her head no. "You Americans! You're still Puritans," he scoffed, but affectionately.

"Middle-class morality."

"Precisely," he said crisply. "With archaic and idealistic ideas about love and marriage."

He looked down at the ring box and turned it over in his hand. His brows lowered in deep concentration. He was remembering something. "Jordan, this decision of yours wouldn't have anything to do with the American journalist, would it?"

"Helmut, how absurd," she said brightly, but ducked her head and turned away so he wouldn't see the pain that flashed in her dull eyes. "Would you like a drink?"

He ignored the offer. "Jordan, look at me." Slowly she complied. He saw the heartsickness that was so clearly etched on her taut features. She held her body rigid and straight, as though if she allowed it to relax it would fly into a million pieces and disintegrate. He let his breath out slowly. "Ahhhh, so *that's* it."

"No, Helmut. He had nothing to do with this." His shrewd skeptical look told her he didn't believe her. "I swear to you that I haven't seen him since we were rescued from the mountain."

"That has very little bearing on your feelings, my dear. Now that I think on it, at that last interview, which Reeves insisted take place that same afternoon, he was in a state of extreme agitation. What happened in that shed where you sought refuge that night?"

"Nothing."

"You're lying, Jordan."

Yes, she was lying. Something *had* happened that night. Her life had begun and ended in the space of those hours she had spent with Reeves. For the past two weeks she had moved through her routine like a programmed automaton, though answering the myriad questions of her customers as patiently and courteously as she could.

Through the maze in her mind, she had tried to map out a plan for her future, since Mr. Bauerman's daughter would soon be arriving to replace her, but she was incapable of thinking beyond one day. Surviving the present required all her effort and concentration.

Now she slumped to the sofa and stared vacantly at her hands. It wasn't until the cushions sank under his weight that she realized Helmut had sat down beside her. He covered her cold hands with both of his. "You're in love with him," he said clairvoyantly.

She nodded miserably. Tears stood in her eyes when she looked up at him. "Helmut, I swear that I had already

174

made up my mind about us before I ever saw Reeves Grant."

"I believe you, but that's hardly the point, is it? Does he know how you feel?"

"No."

"You are a most infuriating creature, Jordan. Why didn't you tell the man? Do you expect him to play guessing games with you?"

"No, Helmut. It wouldn't matter if he knew or not. He . . . he doesn't . . . feel the same for me. We're at cross purposes."

"I find that hard to believe. The man is a fool to leave you. I'll have him recalled immediately."

"No!" she exclaimed, and clutched his arms. "Promise me you won't try to contact him in any way. In a day or so I'll be going home. I'll feel better then."

He looked at her doubtfully. "I only received one letter from him. The magazine story is scheduled for publication early next year. He said he would let me know when."

She hated herself for asking, but couldn't help it. "Where was the letter postmarked?"

"Paris."

She sighed. "Yes, that's where he said he was going."

"Jordan—"

"I'm all right, Helmut. Really I am." She smiled with more bravery than she felt.

After a while she escorted him down the stairs and unlocked the door. He turned and embraced her warmly, kissing her on both cheeks in a typical European gesture. "My dear Jordan. I've enjoyed our time together. It was in this room that I first met you. I'll always feel a pang of nostalgia whenever I walk by this way. Are you sure you won't marry me?"

"Yes, I'm sure," she said patiently. "You've expanded my world, Helmut. My outlook. Knowing you has been an education."

"I'm a prize jackass," he said.

It was so out of character for him to put himself down that Jordan laughed. "Why?"

He hugged her tightly. "I should have bundled you off to bed when I had the chance instead of honoring your objections to the impropriety. I'll never forgive myself."

"It was my constant refusals that kept you intrigued," she said lightly. "Sooner or later you would have given up and gone away."

"Don't be too sure of that," he whispered as his blue eyes studied the lovely face turned up to his. He cleared his throat. "When will you leave?"

"I don't know exactly. Bill is supposed to notify me within a few days."

"May I see you again before you go?" he asked gently.

Her smile was sad. "I don't think so, Helmut. It will be better this way."

"Always pragmatic. Your common sense is one of your virtues, Jordan."

She laughed again. "That isn't a very gallant compliment. Where are all those poetic comments you used to shower me with?"

He laughed, too, but then grew serious. "Don't misunderstand me. Your astute mind didn't diminish your sexual attractiveness." He drew her close one last time and whispered the next words directly in her ear. "Don't let that solid common sense always dictate the course of your life, Jordan. Some of my finest achievements have been the result of a gamble."

He kissed her once on the lips and then he was gone.

"Damn," Jordan muttered as she retraced her footsteps back down the first three stairs. Just a moment before she had closed the shop for the night and turned out the light. Now one last customer was rudely knocking on the door.

She was tired. For the last week she had been trying to get the newsstand in tip-top shape before Bill arrived with the Bauermans. At night, after business hours, she had been packing her personal belongings into shipping crates. Today had been particularly busy. A tour bus of senior citizens from Detroit had descended upon her and all fifty-one of them had demanded personal attention. When they left, her shelves had been depleted and had required restocking.

Now someone was blatantly ignoring her CLOSED sign. In exasperation she turned the key in the lock and jerked the door open. "I'm clo—" The words died on her lips and the blue rings around her gray eyes widened.

Reeves was standing on the threshold. He was leaning nonchalantly on the outside wall. His gaze was taking in the heavy clouds overhead, which just now were letting loose their first raindrops.

"I can't ever seem to get here in anything less than a deluge," he remarked inconsequentially, and shoved his way past her. She was so stunned to see him that she didn't try to keep him out. Instead her jaw hung slack and her arms dangled uselessly at her sides.

"W-what are you doing here?" she wheezed.

177

"I came to help you pack." He plopped his camera case and duffle bag onto the floor and shrugged out of the shearling coat. "Have you got anything to eat? I'm starving."

Without another word, he wheeled around, and a second later she heard his booted footsteps clumping upstairs. Still incredulous over his brazen entrance, she followed him. When she reached the top of the stairs, he was in the kitchen, inspecting the pantries.

"Peanut butter? Is that all?" he asked in disappointment. "I guess we'll have to go out for dinner."

"Reeves?" she grated as her hands balled into aggravated fists. "What are you doing here?"

He looked at her sympathetically. "You're repeating yourself, Jordan. You already asked me that."

"And you didn't answer."

"Yes I did. I told you that I was here to help you pack. You're leaving in a few days, aren't you?"

His easygoing manner as he spread a piece of stale bread with drying peanut butter amazed her. What did he expect of her? She didn't know what he was up to, but she was growing angrier by the moment with this game he was playing.

She yanked the sandwich out of his hands before he could take the first bite and tossed it onto the table. "Reeves, I don't know what you're doing here, but I want no part of it. How dare you come waltzing in here like this!"

She was building up a full head of steam, but he squelched it when he grumbled, "You ruined my sandwich," and pointed to the bread that had landed peanut-butter side down on the butcher-block tabletop. "Are you going to be this cranky after we're married?"

Married! The word bounced off the walls of the minuscule kitchen and fairly screamed through her head. He had totally dismantled her arsenal of self-defense. She sagged weakly against the kitchen counter and watched him with disbelieving eyes. He picked up the gooey sandwich, inspected it, decided it wasn't ruined after all, folded it over once, and took a huge bite out of it.

"You're crazy," she said. "What do you mean by 'married'?"

"You know," he mumbled around the bread and peanut butter. " 'Dearly beloved, we are gathered here,' etcetera, etcetera. Flowers. Candles. Weepy mothers. Married."

"But—"

"You aren't still engaged to Helmut, are you?"

She could only shake her head dumbly.

"I didn't think so. I was walking down the Champs Elysées yesterday and nearly stumbled into a kiosk. Recently I've been drinking quite a bit, you see, and have developed a wavering gait," he added in a confidential tone. "Anyway, there was this scandal sheet with Helmut's picture on the front page. His arm was around the waist of an Italian contessa whose financial assets receive almost as much acclaim as her physical endowments. I invested a few francs and bought the rag. After five cups of scalding black coffee and an icy cold shower, when I was sure I was sober, I read the story. It seems that Helmut and the contessa are going hot and heavy all over Europe. So I figured that you were free to marry me. I think we'll wait till we get back to the States to tie the knot. I know your parents and my mother—"

"Reeves!" she cried. When his running chatter finally

wound down she said calmly, "You can't just come in here and announce that we're getting married."

"Why not? We love each other, don't we?" Then he smacked his forehead with his palm. "Of course! You prefer for me to ask you. Okay." He shrugged. "Will you marry me, Jordan? I'm easy to live with. I've got all my teeth and I don't need root-canal work. I'm strong of body. Fairly sound of mind. I've stopped smoking—twice. I drink only in moderation—the past few weeks don't count. I shower at least once a day. I have a charming personality. I'm devastatingly handsome and—"

"Humble."

He nodded in solemn affirmation. "And humble."

That was her undoing. She began to laugh. He was beside her in one giant step. His arms went around her, entrapping her against his chest. Her hair became tangled between his fingers as he pulled her head back so he could look down into her face. His amusing mien had disappeared, to be replaced by an earnest frown of anxiety.

"Does that mean yes?" he asked.

She didn't think of her unhappy marriage to Charles. She didn't think of her determination to live independently. Her only consideration was that Reeves had come back into her life. After these miserable weeks of living without him, she wasn't about to let him leave again. "How could I possibly refuse such a romantic proposal?"

"You can't. I won't let you." His eyes ravished her face, touching each feature with scorching green eyes. "I've been in hell, Jordan. That night I groped my way to your door through that thunderstorm, I never really thought of being struck by lightning. But I was the moment I saw you. I never counted on falling in love, but when I did it jarred me all the way up to my brain. I've got to have you in my life." His mouth hovered a mere fraction over hers. "God, I've missed you."

Her lips were parted by the urgency of his. His tongue touched hers with that rare familiarity that had stunned them since their first shared kiss. She felt utterly helpless under its tender quest and surrendered to the mastery of his mouth. The desire that she had kept banked for the past few weeks flared to life with this merest fanning of the embers.

Her mouth matched the passion of his, and she delighted him by moving closer and reminding him of the interlocking way their bodies fit together. He responded with a gentle thrust of his hips.

Pulling away from her after long minutes of ravenous kissing, he cradled her head in his palms and looked deep into her eyes. "Jordan, why did you run to Helmut when he met us coming down from the mountain?" His soft voice only intensified the magnitude of the question and his need to hear her answer.

"I couldn't let you see how much I loved you, Reeves. You had just said that you were leaving, going to Paris. I thought you were making a clean break and didn't want me to read any lasting significance into what had happened between us."

"I asked you if you knew what you meant to me. You said you did."

"I thought I had been a pleasant pastime, that you were leaving me with no strings attached."

"You goose," he chided. "If you'll recall, it wasn't a very opportune time or place for me to tell you that I wanted to be with you forever. As soon as I had seen to my business in Paris, I intended to come back for you. I hoped you would infer that. Instead, the next thing I knew you were tearing down the hillside toward Helmut and accepting that damned diamond ring that I had come to loathe."

"Oh, Reeves. Next time don't be so cryptic."

"There'll never be a next time. You've got to marry me now, Jordan," he said insistently as he curved his hands under her hips and drew her to him.

"Why? Are you pregnant?"

He playfully jerked her head back by a fistful of hair. "No, but I'll work very hard at getting you pregnant if that'll guarantee your marrying me," he warned. "As a matter of fact, I rather like that idea. Think of all the pictures I could take of you and the babies."

"Babies?"

"Yes. You know—those tiny little humans who squall and squirm a lot."

"I'm too old to start having babies," she argued.

"Then we'd better get started," he growled as he propelled her toward the bedroom.

"Do you have any reservations about marrying me?" he asked as his lips slowly nibbled the sensitive skin on the underside of her arm.

Their clothes were messily piled on top of half-packed crates and they were nestled in the covers of the bed they had shared once before.

Outside it was raining.

"I have a million reservations," she murmured against his ribs. Her fingertips were traversing the length of his thigh. "But a wise man once told me not to let my common sense make every decision for me. Sometimes one has to take a gamble. I think you're a reasonably good risk."

He placed a finger under her chin and tilted her face up. "This wise man wouldn't be named Helmut Eckherdt by any chance?"

"By chance he was."

"Well, I'll be damned," he chuckled. "Leave it to him to take charge."

"You mean . . ."

"Yes, I heard from him, too. I was furiously packing last night when he called my hotel room. He told me in no uncertain terms that I'd better get my ass in gear and marry you before someone much smarter than I did. When I told him I was on my way here to do just that, he said, 'Good boy,' and hung up."

They laughed together softly. "He always did like to take matters into his own hands."

"I like to take matters into my own hands, too," Reeves said. Only it wasn't "matters" that his hands closed over but the lush mounds of her breasts. She eased over onto her back and provided him with unrestricted freedom. He dipped his head and kissed the deep cleft between her breasts. "You're distracting me," he said.

Instinctively she arched against him and felt his arousal, hard and hot, against her. "From what?" she asked. Her hand found him and implored him to come nearer.

"From telling you about my new job." His voice had an edge to it. "Forget it for now." Instantly he was released and pushed away. He blinked rapidly. "Can't you do what you were doing and listen at the same time?"

"No. Because you can't talk if I keep doing what I was doing."

"Not very articulately anyway. Damn. Well, I'll hurry." He lay his head on her breasts and said, "A publishing house in New York has been after me for years to compile a book, a pictorial essay of sorts, on the last decade, which would encompass most of my career. I went to Paris to meet with some of their top editors who were there for some book fair or some such. Anyway, to make a long story as short as I possibly can—I have *pressing* problems that need to be seen to—we negotiated a contract. How does that sound?"

"Reeves," Jordan cried enthusiastically. She sat up, dislodging his head from its comfortable pillow. "That's wonderful. Are you excited?"

"Yeah," he admitted abashedly. "It will mean a lot of money, but at the same time force me to evaluate how I feel about all the things I've seen, heard, and experienced these last years. Some of those experiences have been invaluable and I think they should be shared. Do you think two writers in one family is too absurd to contemplate?"

She ran her fingers lovingly through his mussed hair. "I think I could survive anything with you. The concept of the book is marvelous. I'll help you all I can."

"Good. I can't spell worth a damn. Now that that's out of the way . . ." He placed his hands on her shoulders and tried to push her back, but she remained upright.

"I'm not finished yet. Where will we live?"

He muttered a soft curse. "I haven't really decided. Are you averse to the Washington, D.C., area? Virginia has some lovely spots." Then, with exaggerated offhandedness, he added, "We have an extremely photogenic

First Family. And year after next will be election time again."

A worried frown creased her brow and darkened the blue rings around the gray irises. "Reeves, you're not going to miss all the travel and excitement, are you?"

He clasped her to him. "No. With my experience and credentials, I'll never be without a job, but the younger shooters can have the globe-hopping. I know how much you want stability and a home. I want that, too. I was serious when I said that I want to take pictures of you and the babies from now on."

She didn't resist this time when he drew her back onto the pillows. "And I was serious when I said I was too old."

"Nonsense. Look at how fit you are." His eyes were analyzing her body with lascivious pleasure. "Absolutely beautiful." His lips followed his eyes. "One of these days I'm going to take the time to count your errogenous zones. It will no doubt take me hours. Lovely hours."

Her breasts were given ardent attention and they responded in a way not disappointing to his lips. "Would you deny a baby the pleasure of feeding on these breasts?" he asked. His tongue brought her nipples to peaks of aching desire and indulged them with the gentle tugging of his mouth. She moaned at the warm, lubricating sensation.

His hands adored her as they descended slowly into that secret realm that nested the very essence of her womanhood. He found her ready and yearning for his touch. When his lips caught up to his hands and he kissed her there, she cried out with the unspeakable joy of loving and knowing she was loved.

"I love you, Jordan," he vowed as he raised himself

over her. Her thighs squeezed against the sinewy muscles of his legs as he settled himself between them. He joined his body to hers.

"Have I convinced you yet that you would be a perfect mother?"

"Convince me some more."

His body stroked hers inside and out, and she rose to meet each seductive motion. His hand slid between their bodies and found her breast. "You have so much love to give, Jordan. Be generous. Have our baby." He cupped her and rubbed her against his own hair-matted flesh.

"Reeves, you know I love you. Make me yours."

"You are mine. Forever." She held him tighter. An answering shudder streaked through his body. "Jordan, I'll never have enough of you."

At that moment her own passion sent her soaring out into the universe, but he was with her, holding her, sharing it. And when she felt the thrilling fire of his loins she knew he was right.

A love such as this deserved an heir.

Silhouette Desire
15-Day Trial Offer
A new romance series that explores contemporary relationships in exciting detail

Four Silhouette Desire romances, free for 15 days!
We'll send you four new Silhouette Desire romances to look over for 15 days, absolutely free! If you decide not to keep the books, return them and owe nothing.

Four books a month, free home delivery. If you like Silhouette Desire romances as much as we think you will, keep them and return your payment with the invoice. Then we will send you four new books every month to preview, just as soon as they are published. You pay only for the books you decide to keep, and you never pay postage and handling.

Coming Next Month

Velvet Touch by Stephanie James

Tawny, elegant Lacey Sheldon was determined to cut loose from her librarian's past and find liberation out west. This island paradise in Puget Sound seemed the perfect place to begin . . . until she met Holt Randolph. He said he didn't want half a heart, and challenged her to gamble it all in a blazing affair that would bring her to her senses—and into his arms.

The Cowboy And The Lady by Diana Palmer

Jace had given Amanda her first taste of passion. His silver eyes had held a forbidden fascination for her, but at sixteen she'd been too inexperienced to understand the fiery message in his searing kisses. Now Amanda was ready to learn the lessons of desire, and there was only one man who could teach her—a man whose glittering gaze held the secrets of her unhappy past and the promise of a golden future.

Silhouette Desire

Coming Next Month

Come Back, My Love by Pamela Wallace

TV newsperson Toni Lawrence was on the fast
track to fame when photographer Theo Chakaris
swept her off her feet at the Royal Wedding. How
had she abandoned herself to this adventurer?
Storybook romances belonged to princes and
princesses. She tried to forget, to bury herself
in her work, but passion brought them
together to recapture the glory of ecstasy.

Blanket Of Stars by Lorraine Valley

Greece was the perfect setting for adventure and
romance. But for Glena Fielding it became more.
This land she would call home. In Alex Andreas'
dark eyes she saw a passion and a glory, a flame to
light her senses and melt her resistance beneath
the searing Greek sun. In his arms she became
invincible as he led her to the stars.

YOU'LL BE SWEPT AWAY
WITH SILHOUETTE DESIRE

$1.75 each

1 ☐ CORPORATE AFFAIR
Stephanie James

2 ☐ LOVE'S SILVER WEB
Nicole Monet

3 ☐ WISE FOLLY
Rita Clay

4 ☐ KISS AND TELL
Suzanne Carey

5 ☐ WHEN LAST WE LOVED
Judith Baker

6 ☐ A FRENCHMAN'S KISS
Kathryn Mallory

7 ☐ NOT EVEN FOR LOVE
Erin St. Claire

8 ☐ MAKE NO PROMISES
Sherry Dee

9 ☐ MOMENT IN TIME
Suzanne Simms

10 ☐ WHENEVER I LOVE YOU
Alana Smith

Silhouette Desire

Now Available

Not Even For Love by Erin St. Claire

When a misunderstanding threatened to drive them apart, the memory of their passion drove Jordan to convince Reeves of the truth. His misty green eyes and sensual mouth had lifted her to peaks of ecstasy she could never forget.

Make No Promises by Sherry Dee

Even though Cassie was engaged to another man, she was instantly attracted to Steele Malone. He waged a passionate war on her senses, defying her emotions and lulling her body with primitive pleasures.

Moment In Time by Suzanne Simms

She knew Tyler expected a man to build his treasured dam, but Carly was a fully qualified civil engineer. What began as a battle of wills blazed anew in the Santa Fe sunset, a flashfire passion which consumed them both.

Whenever I Love You by Alana Smith

Diana Nolan was Treneau Cosmetics' new goddess of beauty. Paul Treneau was the boss who whisked her away to his Hawaiian paradise for "business." But she had ignited in him a spark of desire fated to burn out of control.

Enjoy your own special time with Silhouette Romances.

Send for 6 books today— one is yours __free__!

Silhouette Romances take you into a special world of thrilling drama, tender passion, and romantic love. These are enthralling stories from your favorite romance authors—tales of fascinating men and women, set in exotic locations all over the world.

Convenient free home delivery. We'll send you six exciting Silhouette Romances to look over for 15 days. If you enjoy them as much as we think you will, pay the invoice enclosed with your trial shipment. **One book is yours free to keep.** Silhouette Romances are delivered right to your door with never a charge for postage or handling. There's no minimum number of books to buy, and you may cancel at any time.

Silhouette Romances